ROMANCING THE GRAVESTONE

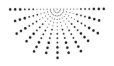

GENA SHOWALTER
JILL MONROE

AUTHOR TALK MEDIA

Cover Created by Leni Kauffman

Editing by AZ Editing

Proofreading by Naomi Lane

The following images through Depositphotos.com:

Chapter Header: chempina

Ornamental Breaks: esancai

Thank you to our families for their endless encouragement and our pets who inspire us.

·

Special thanks to Ginny at AZ Editing.

·

Thanks also goes to Leni Kauffman who captured Jane perfectly in her cover design.

·

Much love to Naomi Lane for keeping us on track.

·

A shout out to Lauren Floyd and everyone on our reader team. You guys ROCK!

CHAPTER ONE

Edward Jacobs
I don't have time for death. I'll be back soon.
Plot 47, Garden of Memories

*J*ane Ladling brushed her bangs aside and peered into the fresh grave. Her mind whirled, different observations hitting her. Plot 39. Six-foot hole. Open casket. Pretty standard for the Garden of Memories, a private cemetery she'd inherited from her mother's side of the family. Except this resident had been underground for the better part of a century, in a closed casket, alone. Someone—or some*ones*—had redug the pit, unsealed his final resting place and given him a friend.

Two of the dead pressed chest to chest. It was almost…beautiful. *Should I make couples coffins a new thing?*

They just looked so peaceful together. If you ignored the fact that Rhonda Burgundy, the older resident, was nothing but hair and bone. Honestly? She looked better than the new guy who still had flesh and blood.

Was this the afterlife's version of robbing the cradle?

Bad Jane. Bad! Focus. How had this happened? Accident? Foul play? She'd been walking the grounds, doing her morning chores, when she'd noticed an unauthorized pile of dirt and hurried over.

Now, she rocked back on her heels and cast her gaze over the surrounding plots, trying to make sense of everything. Morning sunshine drenched plush green grass. Shade cast by a full-figured magnolia tree and a scattering of cypresses bathed different headstones. A row of smaller, moss-covered cypresses lined a babbling brook. Flowers bloomed here and there, drawing a handful of bees. Nothing appeared disturbed, but honestly, Jane doubted the newcomer had died of natural causes.

She had a perfect view of his back. Droplets of crimson matted his hair. A cap of blond curls she thought she might recognize. Maybe? Possibly? *So familiar.*

Her coworker, Rolex, weaved through her feet. Rolex-speak for *Feed me, peasant.* In exchange for room and board, he deigned to watch over Jane and the property. He also worked as the resident meal inspector.

Two years ago, the little house panther had wandered into the cemetery and promptly declared his ownership of it, as well as of Jane. They'd been together ever since.

"Breakfast needs to wait, baby. For the both of us. I've got to tell the sheriff about our squatter."

Jane, who'd been compiling her to-do list for the day, had to quit halfway for the first time. She turned on the heels of her black flats and headed home. A two-story caretaker's cottage, aka ancestral estate, that dated back multiple generations and bordered the cemetery.

Having spent the bulk of her twenty-six years here, tending gravesites, she'd developed what the good folks of Aurelian Hills, Georgia called "an inability to grasp the gravity of death." Perhaps they were right. But why mourn the dead? Most times, they made better friends than the living.

As Jane trekked over the rolling hills and beautiful grounds she preserved in pristine condition, Rolex kept pace at her side. A fragrant bouquet of magnolia, gardenia and rose blossoms perfumed the warm spring air. Her favorite collection of scents in the world. All too soon, new aromas would weave into the mix. Car exhaust. A plethora of colognes and perfumes. Stale coffee, probably. And the sounds! The damage! Law enforcement—or rather, the living, the bane of Rolex's existence—would trek all over the place.

"On second thought, breakfast should not be delayed. You'll be too busy hissing and swiping your murder mittens at everyone to eat." His way of letting visitors know they had no right to breathe *his* air in *his* kingdom without *his* permission.

Boards groaned as she ascended the porch steps, and hinges creaked as she opened the door. A familiar symphony. She kept the cottage updated as much as possible, but funds were tight, and the biggest, most needful repairs had yet to be completed. Or started. One day!

In the foyer, she paused as she always paused when faced with Grandma Lily's furnishings. The orange velvet sofa, with a hand-knitted blanket draped over the side. The floral print chairs flanking the unlit hearth, where all that knitting had taken place. The coffee table with hundreds of Jane's accidental nicks. *Love spots*, according to her grandmother.

Three years had passed since the cancer had taken Grandma Lily. With every fiber of Jane's being, she missed the dear woman who'd raised her. No one had been kinder, or more encouraging.

Rolex meowed at her feet, pulling her from her reverie.

"All right, all right. Let's make you less inclined to commit a felony today. One a day is enough." In the kitchen, she opened a new tube of chicken pâté and squeezed the disgusting blob onto the cat's dish.

Rolex dove in. He loved the stuff and refused to approve of anything else.

When she'd first found him, he'd been outside, half starved, sitting atop a jar of pickles she'd tossed out the day before. The jar had fallen to the ground right side up and he'd perched on the lid, reminding her of a gargoyle atop a castle, guarding his territory. Her initial thought—watch cat. Her second—Rolex. She barely remembered her grandpa, but she'd never forgotten his obsession with the wristwatch he'd touted as "pure luxury."

She washed and dried her hands, then headed to the office at the back of the house. The room was an addition Pops had added just before he'd died fifteen years ago. Because of his arthritic hips, he hadn't enjoyed walking to the main office on the other side of the property, near the cemetery's entrance.

Jane preferred this workspace, anyway. The spacious room contained an elaborate antique desk, metal filing cabinets filled with records she'd begun logging digitally last year —only three hundred more to go—and framed photos of her favorite people. Grandma Lily and Pops. Rolex, of course. Fiona Lawrence, her grandmother's best friend. Truth be told, the sixty-two-year-old was Jane's best friend, too.

There was a single image of Jane's mother and father, from their high school graduation. Oh yes, and there was also a gilt-framed cross-stitched Henry Cavill that Jane purchased at a garage sale. What? The twenty dollars she'd spent was well worth it, considering they'd been dating in her mind for a year. Her longest relationship to date!

After locating the file for plot 39, she phoned the non-emergency number to the sheriff's department to explain the situation. Unsurprisingly, the head law enforcement officer answered the call himself. As a former mining town, Aurelian Hills boasted roughly ten thousand citizens and employed only a sheriff and his deputy. There was no need for anyone else. Other than the occasional teen swiping makeup at the drugstore or a tourist skipping out on their bill at the Golden Spoon—the best diner in all the world— people tended to behave themselves. The crime rate remained low.

Sheriff Raymond Moore muttered something unintelligible under his breath. "Who is this again?"

"Jane. Jane Ladling. Um...the Cemetery Girl?" A nickname she'd received in elementary school. "I mean, the Cemetery Girl. A statement, not a question. I know who I am."

"Are you sure you saw a body and not a blow-up doll or something, Jane? Kids like to play pranks nowadays."

"Well, there's blood, so... But no, I didn't touch the body to verify my initial observation. Just give me an hour to haul a ladder to the site and—"

"No. Forget it. No ladder, and no touching. I'll be right out to check things out for myself." He heaved a sigh. "This had to happen now, didn't it?" he grumbled. To himself? "I'm due to retire in a matter of weeks and—" Click. The line went dead.

The (seemingly) gruff grandfather of eight had been planning his retirement for the past six years. He'd become an Aurelian Hills staple, and Jane couldn't imagine the town without him. He often passed out Safety Citizen badges to elementary school kids, gave stern lectures about the dangers of drinking or texting while driving to middle and high schoolers, and rushed to the rescue for any and every disaster, ready to utilize his solid strength or offer a comforting presence.

5

Jane exited the house, emerging onto the wraparound porch complete with a sitting area and a swing. She kept the screen door open, ensuring Rolex had optimal viewing of the coming proceedings.

Standing at the wood rail, she waited, serenaded by chirping crickets and buzzing locusts. About half an hour later, the sheriff rolled up in his black-and-white, parked in her gravel driveway, and climbed from the car. Sunlight glinted from his bald head. A full silver beard covered his jaw. Broad shoulders led to a barrel chest and lean hips.

His familiar, grim face loosened surprising stress knots between her shoulder blades. But then, something about his grizzled expression and hard jaw had always eased her. If only Fiona were here. Jane's dearest friend had a love of gossip—er, information and harbored a secret crush on the widower. One she'd nursed for years.

"Take me to the body," he said, withdrawing a small notepad and a pen from the pocket of his button-down.

"Yes, of course." Getting straight to business. Excellent. "Plot 39 is in Autumn Grove. This way."

After blowing Rolex a kiss, she led the sheriff along a cobblestone path.

"Don't you have a golf cart we can use?" the sheriff asked, already huffing and puffing a little.

"Disturb the peace of the grounds and its residents? For shame!" Caretakers of the Garden of Memories had relied on their own two legs for five generations, *not* motorized vehicles, and Jane wasn't about to change things up. Her grandmother would flip in her grave.

"The employees of Aurelian Hills Cemetery use golf carts," he groused.

Aurelian Hills Cemetery. Her fiercest competition and the only other cemetery in town.

Hot-button alert! Jane didn't care. She lifted her nose and

6

jutted her chin. "The employees of Aurelian Hills Cemetery treat their dead the same way they treat the living—horribly. I wouldn't bury a goldfish in their plots."

"My apologies." The sheriff swiped a handkerchief over his sweat-glistened brow. "Didn't mean to offend." He hurried to return to business. "Did you notice anything out of the ordinary this morning?"

"Not until I crested the hill and spied the mound of fresh dirt."

"A mound of dirt isn't standard fare for you?"

"With the town growing around us, we're landlocked," she reminded him. No new plots meant no new residents. "Our last occupant moved in about six years ago."

The Garden of Memories consisted of seventy-five acres of history and beauty, and she loved every inch. Opened soon after Georgia's gold rush, the land boasted ornate crypts, elaborate mausoleums, and angelic sculptures. There was even an arched bridge that bisected a babbling brook, adding a sense of mysticism. Trees, bushes and flowers abounded. Everything from wisteria to maple.

When they reached their destination, Sheriff Moore peered down the six-foot hole and whistled. "Well, I'll be darned. You know who this is?"

"Yes, sir. That's Rhonda Burgundy, and she—"

"Not the corpse. Well, not the old one."

Oh. "Unfortunately, no. I mean, there's a niggle in the back of my brain, but I'm not sure what it means. Do *you* know who this is?"

"Not yet, but I have a niggle, too." He scrubbed a hand over his weary features. "Whoever it is, townsfolk are about to revolt. There hasn't been a murder since I took over for Sheriff Bollersox."

He'd taken over, what? Fifteen years ago? "What makes you suspect foul play? What if the poor guy tripped and fell?"

He'd trespassed in the middle of the night. His vision had been limited. The creepy setting and sounds might have spooked him. But why raid the coffin in the first place? To steal the bones?

"Did you catch someone trespassing?" he asked, ignoring her questions. "Spot someone lurking around?"

"I didn't hear any digging, no." The gravesite was too far from her cottage. "I didn't see anyone lurking around, either. Oh, and in case you're wondering, I usually finish my evening rounds at eight p.m." Her cheeks burned a little bit. How had she not known what was happening on her own land? Especially someone who'd hung out long enough to dig a six-foot hole. "Do you suspect foul play?" she asked again.

The sheriff opened his mouth, as if he planned to respond, only to close it with a snap. "I'm sorry, but I can't discuss details about an open case with you, Miss Ladling."

Understandable. *Had* foul play occurred? "The ladder is in the work shed. I'll fetch it so you can get a closer look."

"Thank you. I phoned GBH on the way over, just in case. As soon as they get my update, they'll head this way."

Georgia Bureau of Homicide. For a potential murder. This was getting serious. "I'll be right back." Except, she took forever. The ladder was heavy, and the trek was long. An hour passed before she made the trek back to the cottage to await the agents.

Her plan? Escort them to the site to prevent any destruction of her lawn.

Jane hurried, the hem of her purple dress dancing around her thighs. She always wore a dress when walking the grounds. As a little girl, she'd adored the fancy clothes worn by funeral attendees, and she'd followed suit. The habit had stuck. Though she preferred bright colors to black. To her, a cemetery wasn't a place of mourning but celebration.

Uh-oh. A dark SUV waited in her winding driveway. An

older guy in the process of removing a GBH jacket stood beside the vehicle while someone in a dark gray suit knocked on her door—two hard rasps from knuckles seemingly made of steel. Rolex growled and batted at the mesh screen that separated them.

"Hi. Hello," she called, waving as she picked up the pace. "You're looking for me."

Both men turned, facing her. Oh wow. Gaze zeroed in on the tall, muscular prime cut beef on her porch, she stopped. Her eyes went wide. Thick dark hair framed a solid, rugged face. Sunglasses obscured the color of his irises, but not the prominent brows above them. He had a strong nose, bronze skin and a thicker-than-normal five o'clock shadow, a combination lethal to good sense. A gun rested at his hip, and a badge gleamed from his belt. A watch circled a strong wrist. And just when had she started noticing wrists? *Anyway*. He was without a tie, his collar unbuttoned. Business casual on hormone supplements.

Thoughts began to derail, speeding down wrong roads. When the singles in Aurelian Hills spotted him, he would get mobbed. Guaranteed. Of course, the singles mobbed anyone, since the pickings in town were so slim. Jane herself hadn't been on a date in…yikes! A year? A tourist had asked her out, and she'd said yes because she'd envisioned a fun night with friendly conversation and multiple laughs. As soon as he'd learned about the cemetery, he'd launched into nonstop questions about dead bodies and things to do with them. There hadn't been a second outing.

A couple other guys had invited her to dinner, but she'd declined. Why bother? She already knew how any relationship would end—at the mercy of the Ladling curse.

A shudder racked her at the mere thought. Family legend stated "a seed was sown in another's field, and now the Ladling women must reap the harvest." In other words, a

Ladling ancestor had seduced another woman's husband, ensuring the Ladling women were forever fated to lose their loves.

The claim had proven itself true in every generation. Ladling sons married and thrived while the females died alone. Jane's mother was dumped by her father right before Jane's birth. Though Grandma Lily wasn't a Ladling by blood, she'd lost her husband far too soon; a heart attack took out Pops in a matter of hours. Her great-grandmother had lost her husband a year after the wedding.

Jane wanted to refute the curse, but how could she? No Ladling woman in recorded history had kept a partner. Not even the duds had stuck around.

Her senior year of high school, Jane certainly hadn't kept a guy. She'd thought she'd fallen head over heels for Clint Lennox, son of the best baker in town. He'd spent a solid year romancing her, only to ghost her a month after graduation. Then had come Christopher, a hotshot fireman who'd dumped her after two months. Apparently, the curse had kicked into hyperdrive for Jane, who seemed to have a thing for men with C names.

"Ma'am?"

The gruff voice snapped her out of her head. *Dead body. Crime. Focus.* She leveled her attention at the man near the SUV. The one who'd spoken. He had salt-and-pepper hair, tanned, weathered skin and a rotund stomach. He dressed more casually than his partner, pairing a blue-collared shirt with khakis.

"I'm Jane Ladling." She held out her hand, and they shook. "I'm the owner and operator of Garden of Memories, where your loved ones rest in beauty as well as peace." She winced. The company motto? Really? "Sorry. Habit."

"No worries. I'm Special Agent Tim Barrow." His neutral

expression gave nothing away. "We're told you found a body."

"Yes. That's me. I'm the finder."

Porch babe jogged down the steps. His long stride ate up the space, and her breath hitched. *Sorry, Henry. There's a new man in my life.*

Forget this dude's amazing good looks, though. The moment he stepped within sniffing distance, she noticed the most incredible scent. Dry cedar and refined spice.

And he smells good, too? How was that even fair to the females of the world? Already she craved a fresh hit each day forever and probably for weeks after.

No wonder he was the one selected to bang on her door. Who *wouldn't* tell this man their deepest, darkest secrets?

"Ma'am." He held out his hand, the sleeve of his jacket lifting, revealing a close-up of his watch—a Rolex—and the hint of a tattoo. How…delicious. Though she tried, she couldn't identify the image.

Wait. Did he call her *ma'am* too? "I'm Jane Ladling." She trembled as her fingers met his. Skin to skin. The heat! The roughness of his palm roused goose bumps. "This is my place." She covered her uncharacteristic reaction to him by (expertly) faking a cough. The burn in her cheeks meant nothing. Everyone knew sunburns could come and go. "The cat is Rolex, in case you were wondering. He is the employee of the month." Again.

"Rolex?" he asked, briefly tracing his fingers over his watch.

"Because he's the world's best watch cat. And don't bother trying to win him over. He's never going to like you. Not that you want to develop a relationship with my cat." Moving on. "You want to see the dead body, I'm sure. I mean, I'm guessing he's dead. I didn't check for a pulse." Was she rambling? It felt as if she rambled.

"I'm Special Agent Ryan. I'd like to ask you a few questions first." His voice was as wonderfully rough as his features, but also as smooth as molasses. The contradiction was kind of maddening.

"So, um, nice to meet you. I mean, not nice, since someone died and all. But, um, yes. Also nice. Because you're a great person. Or I'm guessing you're great. I don't really know you. You might kick puppies in your spare time." *Shutting up now.*

Special Agent Ryan canted his head to the side, as if he'd just deepened his study of her. Had he? Those glasses hid everything except his intensity. Tim Barrow had been deadpan, but this guy took it to a whole new level. Not a single twitch gave away his emotions. "You're the woman who found the victim?"

"Yes. That's me. I was making my morning rounds, planning my chores for the day, when I came across a disturbed plot." She waved to the cobblestone path. "Sheriff Moore is there now. Why don't I answer your questions along the way?"

Jane executed a sharp turn, if only for a reprieve. She marched off, expecting the men to follow. Which they did. Special Agent Barrow remained a few feet behind, but Special Agent Ryan's long stride kept him a little too close for comfort. He was so tall he towered over her. She'd never felt so tiny. Or flustered. Maybe she should have worn heels instead of flats?

As they walked along the grounds, he questioned her about the cemetery and her role here. Unlike most people who learned her occupation, he didn't shrink back as if she had just crawled from one of the graves.

"When we're done at the site," Special Agent Ryan said, "I'd like a copy of your security feed."

Oh, um… "Yes. About that. I absolutely, one hundred

percent, will give you all the security feed I have. Which are my handwritten notes. A to-do list, really. I wrote it as I made my rounds."

He shot her an incredulous look, as if she'd just admitted to robbing three banks and eating the cash. "You live alone in a cemetery and you have no cameras?"

"In my defense, it's a small town. I really only deal with trespassers in October, so there's not a reason to pay for..." She trailed off, stutter-stepping as he pivoted in front of her and removed his sunglasses.

Whiskey. His eyes were the color of her Pops's favorite whiskey and a thousand times more intoxicating. Jane gulped.

He stared down at her, hard, before offering her a slow, lazy smile that didn't reach any of his other features. She expected a stern talking to about her lack of safety. Instead, he nodded. "Thank you for the escort. I need to examine the site without you, however. Please return to the house with Special Agent Barrow." Sliding his sunglasses back into place, he walked away.

The other agent moved to her side, nodding as he did so. "Ma'am," he said with a chilly undertone.

Chilly? But why? The agents didn't think she was guilty, did they? She owned the cemetery for goodness sakes; to hide a body, she had only to fill the hole. No one would have known. Not that she'd ever planned a murder or anything. Although, if she were honest, she would admit she'd had a passing thought here and there. But only out of curiosity.

Anyway. What if the agents believed she was twisted enough to kill someone? No, surely not. What reason did she have? Other than playing cat and mouse games with the authorities. Or stroking her own ego by inserting herself into the investigation. Or boredom. Or ridding herself of an enemy. Good gracious! The reasons were unending.

She gulped with more force and watched Special Agent Ryan. As he spoke with Sheriff Moore, he kept Jane in profile, as if he expected her to strike again.

Oh yes. He and his partner suspected she was twisted enough to do the deed and phone it in, no doubt about it.

CHAPTER TWO

Lucy Edgefield
Here Lies the Best Gold Digger
Plot 9, Garden of Memories

*H*ours passed, each one more excruciating than the last. Special Agent Ryan remained at the crime scene while Special Agent Barrow kept Jane within sight. They sat on the porch together. She occupied the swing, sipping sweet tea, pretending to be at ease while he guzzled coffee in Fiona's rocker and grilled her with questions. He wanted to know everything. Her routine. Her relationships. Her morning—and night—activities. And he wrote her every word inside a notepad, ready to use it all against her at a later date.

Not that it would do him any good. There was nothing incriminating about The Cemetery Girl. Her nightlife comprised of snuggles with Rolex and rereading her favorite romance novels about military men with secrets and warriors with centuries-old grudges. Sometimes she tried on the hats she'd bought at a resale shop or crafters on Etsy. At other times, she worked on her latest knitting project with Fiona.

Eventually, a sedan with new agents arrived. A ginormous truck pulled up only minutes later, the words Georgia Bureau of Homicide decorating its sides. Three other agents exited. A white coroner's van entered the property soon after that.

Her beautiful grass! Jane swallowed whimper after whimper, dining on a full seven courses of air. People with bulky equipment trekked everywhere. Booted feet trampled everything.

Why hadn't she set up shop in the main office, at the front of the property?

Someone died, Jane. Whatever damage her little paradise on Earth sustained could be fixed. But oh, she longed to be out there, directing traffic. No one knew the layout of the land better.

None of the new arrivals ventured to the house to ask questions, at least. Special Agent Barrow gathered the stack of maps Jane had given him, excused himself and strode off to confer with the newcomers. She'd have to remember to order more maps from the printer, a stretch to her already-stretched budget.

When the last agent wandered off, Special Agent Barrow remained in the driveway, pacing. Were more agents due to arrive?

Trepidation prickled the back of her neck. Time for a distraction. "Would you like more coffee?" she called.

"No, thank you." He paced at a faster clip.

Her ears twitched as tires crunched over gravel. Yep. Another arrival. She shaded her eyes and peered down the drive. A bright-red convertible. Fiona!

Special Agent Barrow stiffened, and Jane rushed to stand at the railing.

The (almost) old woman parked beside Jane's vehicle, which just happened to be a hearse. First of all, the car had come with the business. Second, Pops had been a mechanic at heart, and he'd rebuilt the engine himself, ensuring she couldn't bear to part with the thing. Ever. Third, it was a Cadillac. The best vehicle ever made, according to Grandma Lily and Fiona.

Fiona eased out, gaping at the fleet of vehicles before marching up the porch steps. The world's most amazing woman was petite and curvy, with a short cap of black curls and dark skin. The only lines she bore were those she'd earned with love and laughter.

"Jane Ladling, you tell me what's going on right this second. Then you tell me why I didn't receive a call right when this mess started? Whatever this mess is. Are you all right? Are you hurt? Or in trouble?"

"I'm fine, I promise." The trouble, though…

"Ma'am," Special Agent Barrow said in greeting, even while extending his arm to warn Fiona away. "This isn't a good time to visit. Come back later this evening."

"She's with me," Jane told him, ready to fly down there and *handle this* if necessary. "She's my family."

Special Agent Barrow hesitated before offering a clipped nod.

Fiona humphed as she passed him.

"Have a seat." Fighting a grin, Jane kissed her friend on the cheek. "I'll get you a glass of tea and tell you everything that's happened."

"Yes, you most certainly will tell me everything." A chiding tone couldn't mask her friend's continued concern. "You should have alerted me right away about the trouble you're having."

"Next time I will, promise." Next time? Jane winced as she rushed inside to the kitchen. The air conditioner was set ten

degrees higher than her friend's age—an incomparable 72—
yet her damp, overheated body reacted as if she'd entered an
arctic blast, shivering uncontrollably. As fast as possible, she
selected Fiona's favorite twelve-ounce glass from the
cupboard, poured peach schnapps to the half-way point and
added two splashes of sweet tea. Her friend's special mix.

Rolex had taken a break from guard duty and now slept
on the table, curled in the centerpiece—an empty bowl. The
excitement of the day had exhausted him.

When she returned to the porch, a sizzling breeze
enveloped her, making her miss the cold. Fiona already
perched in her rocker. Jane reclaimed her spot on the swing,
to the left of her friend.

Today, Fiona wore her typical attire: a colorful blouse,
loose slacks, and a chunky necklace. "Tell me everything,
hon. Leave nothing out."

The endearment made her chest clench every time. The
same endearment Grandma Lily had used.

A consummate gossip—sorry, *information gatherer*—the
retired school teacher liked to say, "If you don't know what
you're doing, someone else will."

Jane explained the circumstances, withholding only two
minor details that had no bearing on the situation whatsoever. Special Agent Ryan's appearance and her reaction to
him hardly mattered at all, really.

Her friend's eyes widened. "The dead man is blond, you
say? Well, butter my butt and call me a biscuit. I'm solving
the murder even as we speak. This morning, Tiffany
Hotchkins, Dr. Hotchkins's wife—do you know her? She's
about your age, I think. Twenty-six. Maybe twenty-seven.
Anyway, she posted on the Headliner, asking if anyone had
seen or heard from her husband."

The AH Headliner, also known as "the Headliner" and
"the Head's Up." An app used by town members to share

recipes and exchange theories about everything going on in everyone's life. Marriages. Divorces. Social events. Scandals. Issue guesses about the secret ingredient in a certain someone's famous blueberry pancakes. And okay, yes, maybe Jane was the only one who'd ever posted about that last one. So what? The most popular section was known as Panning for Dates.

"If that's not enough to wet your whistle," Fiona continued, "Sandy Whitaker also posted. She had an appointment with Dr. Garcia bright and early this morning. You see him too, don't you? She said the office was packed to the brim, with poor Dr. Garcia sprinting from room to room, covering both his and Dr. Hotchkins's patients."

Dr. Hotchkins. Also known as Dr. Hots. Some of his patients sometimes invented various ailments to see him. Jane flipped through mental files and found his photo. Late forties. A little over six feet tall. Lean. A full cap of blond hair. He and Dr. Garcia ran the local clinic.

Jane's thoughts whirled. Marcus Hotchkins certainly fit the victim's description, now that she thought about it. Well, what she'd seen of his back fit, anyway. She'd never really interacted with the man personally. He'd only moved to town a few years ago. Once or twice she'd caught sight of him and his mop of blond waves when she'd visited Dr. Garcia. She'd also attended high school with his wife. They'd run with different crowds, though. Tiffany came from one of the town's wealthiest families. She'd been head cheerleader, beloved by all, while Jane had been president of the book club and ignored by most.

"I've never liked Dr. Hotchkins," Fiona continued. Her expression shifted, as if she'd just smelled something rotten. "I've caught him eyeing my tush on more than one occasion, thank you very much!"

"Doesn't *every* man check out your tush?"

"You aren't wrong, hon." Fiona fluffed her hair. "But the doctor… He's got himself a roving eye. I bet he dabbled with someone he shouldn't and a jealous husband or boyfriend decided to whack him."

The theory intrigued Jane, her curiosity fully engaged. Why *had* someone killed a well-respected doctor? If the dead man was, in fact, Dr. Hotchkins. What little she knew about him came from gossip, and no one agreed. A nice man. But also a not nice man. Charming and also off-putting. She remembered there'd been a big to do after he'd married Tiffany and moved into her ancestral estate. A mansion atop the hill that overlooked the entire city.

She darted her gaze to Special Agent Barrow, who still paced in the driveway. Leaning closer, she whispered, "Should we tell the agents about our suspicion?"

Fiona wiggled her nose, as if to say, *Those amateurs?* "We know more than they do. They'll only add our names to the suspect list. No, thank you."

Too late. "I think I top the list already."

"You *what?*" Fiona gasped out. "Oh no, no, no. No! That is unacceptable. We're gonna prove your innocence to those fools."

Excitement bloomed and grew. Yes! She could absolutely prove her innocence. Which should be easy, considering she was, in fact, innocent. "I know just where to start. Excuse me a moment." Bordering on giddy, she rushed inside the house to unearth the kind of notepad Sheriff Moore and the agents carried. Jane could keep track of her investigation, too. Better safe than sorry.

She returned to the swing beside Fiona to write down her thoughts and findings.

"Well?" Fiona prompted, exasperated. "Where do we start?"

"With a notebook." She waved the pad in the woman's direction. "Where else? I'm calling this one Truth Be Told."

"Oh, good grief. They say we shouldn't despise small beginnings, but girl, this might be the smallest beginning of all." Her friend shifted, ice cubes clinking in her glass. "Just out of curiosity and no other reason, did Sheriff Moore happen to ask about me when he arrived? No, don't tell me. I'm not ready to know. Not about him. Although it probably wouldn't hurt to check in on him at the murder site. No, never mind. I don't go to men; men come to me. Besides, I'd rather hear about you and why you didn't call me the second you stumbled upon trouble."

Jane fought a grin. "I was waiting until I had more information. I knew you'd have questions, and I wanted to be able to answer as many as possible."

Fiona sipped her tea. "Not a terrible excuse, I suppose. But not a great one, either."

A grin began to spread. From the corner of her eye, Jane noticed the approach of Special Agent Ryan.

Her breath caught, and she sat up straighter. Her heart thumped double time. Triple time! At some point during his examination of the scene, he'd rolled up his shirtsleeves to reveal powerful forearms covered with tattoos and smears of dirt. He'd removed his watch and his sunglasses, his expression as hard as granite. Uh-oh. Her stomach twisted, and her pulse leaped. What did this mean?

"And who is *this*?" Fiona purred for her ears alone, sitting up straighter as well.

"No one. Someone. The other agent." Her cheeks burned hotter than before.

"Ms. Ladling, I'd like a word," he said with a smooth smile. Practiced? The delivery of the invitation might drip with charm, but there was no mistaking his command.

Shivers cascaded over her spine. No, not shivers, but

fresh shudders. This wasn't a good thing, but bad. Very, very bad. "Do I need a lawyer?" she asked, wringing her hands.

He pounded up the porch steps and paused, his eyes narrowing. "I don't know. Do you?"

Okay, wrong approach. She stood and smoothed the lines of her fit and flare. "I didn't do the crime, so I shouldn't do the time. Right? Unless there isn't a crime?" Other than trespassing and grave tampering. "Did Dr. Hotchkins trip and fall or something?"

Special Agent Ryan blinked with surprise. "How did you identify the victim if you couldn't see his face?"

First, this was confirmation that they'd guessed correctly. How sweet was that? Second, big dang. Had she just confirmed his earlier suspicions? "We—*I* put two and two together. Curly blond hair on the corpse. Missing doctor with curly blond hair." No reason to involve Fiona unless absolutely necessary. "There's only one fair-haired doctor people can't currently find."

"Small towns have the biggest mouths," he muttered. "We'll be taking both bodies as well as the casket."

"Have you already dusted it for fingerprints? Never mind. You can't say. I get it. Before you ask, I've never spoken to Dr. Hots. Hotchkins," she corrected. "I mean, I've spotted him a few times when I visited Dr. Garcia. And I know his wife. But other than that, I have zero connection to him." *Okay, you can shut up now.*

"Good to know." He pulled out his little notebook to make a notation. "We're packing up to leave, but I'd like to discuss something with you before I go." He slid his gaze to Fiona and offered his hand. "I'm Special Agent Ryan. If you'll excuse us for a moment, I'd appreciate it."

Oh, introductions might be nice. "Sorry. Special Agent Ryan, this is Fiona Lawrence, my best friend."

Fiona glanced between them, smiling with pure, undiluted calculation. "Are you single, young man? I see no wedding ring. Perhaps you have a significant other?"

His expression remained unchanged. "Were you at the house this morning, ma'am?"

"I wasn't. Let's get out of this heat, and I'll tell you what I *was* doing. I'll even whip up a batch of my famous blueberry pancakes. At some point, I might explain the impoliteness of ignoring an old woman's question. Although I've already deduced the answer. You are *very* single."

He canted his head. A slow process, as if he were considering a thousand responses at once. "What makes you think so?"

"The eyes," Fiona said. "The eyes always give you away."

"Thank you for the tip." His gaze slid to Jane, and her cheeks burned.

Forget Fiona's obvious attempt at matchmaking, which was a common occurrence. Those blueberry pancakes were ambrosia, with a unique ingredient no one could figure out. Her guess? Crack. No food in history had ever tasted as amazing as those pancakes. And that wasn't hyperbole. Jane would absolutely commit a murder to steal a triple stack. Problem was, Fiona prepared the sweet treat for only three reasons. And those reasons always changed, according to her agenda.

"Yes," she blurted out. "He wants those pancakes. Please say yes." *Please.* If he had the slightest sliver of a heart, he would agree.

"I'm sorry, but I don't have time," he said. "There are too many other places I need to be today."

His hotness chilled fast. "You fool," she muttered, only realizing she'd said the words aloud. Her cheeks might have actually caught flame. Thankfully, he didn't seem to hear her words or witness her mortification.

On the other hand, Fiona frowned at him, as if disappointed in his character, his life choices and even his next breath.

"Uh, you mentioned you wanted to discuss something with me?" Jane asked.

"Yes. I'd like a list of names. Everyone buried in Autumn Grove and any of their visitors for the past month."

"Have you been to a cemetery lately? We open the gates, and people come in. I give directions if someone has trouble finding their loved one, but that's about it for public interaction."

He made a notation in his notepad. "Anyone can wander around unsupervised, at any given time?" he asked with the slightest hint of censure.

"Well, yes. Kind of. People visit their loved ones to reflect on the past when the urge strikes, when time allows and for any number of reasons. This is a cemetery, after all, not a bank ripe for a heist."

Another notation. Another charming but humorless smile. "I'll take any records you have."

What was his deal? "Yes, of course. I've already pulled the file. We're happy to hand it over, along with anything else you need. Or want." No. She had *not* just added that.

"I'll copy the file," Fiona offered as she lumbered to her feet. She'd learned the business at Grandma Lily's side, and she'd even helped train Jane. "You stay here chatting with the nice agent, hon. It's perfectly proper, since you're *both* very single. Isn't that right, Special Agent Ryan? Did I guess correctly or do I need to stay and chaperone?"

He pursed his lips, but said, "No chaperone needed, ma'am."

"Well. See how easy it is to be polite?" With a wink, she sauntered into the house.

Oh, dear Lord save me. The embarrassment never ended.

Special Agent Ryan scrubbed a hand over his mouth, as if wiping away a grin.

Unlike Jane, Fiona didn't believe in the curse. For years she'd tried to set up the widowed Lily on dates. When Lily died, she'd turned her sights on Jane. But Jane wasn't interested. Why start something with a doomed, predetermined ending?

The agent exchanged his notepad for a map of the cemetery. "Are there any unmarked entry points into Autumn Grove?"

"There are," Jane said with a nod, "but I kind of need to *show-you* show you. Which I'm happy to do. Let me grab a hat." A harsh afternoon glare had replaced the soft morning sunlight, and Jane burned easily. "I'll be right back. Don't leave without me!" She shot from his overwhelming presence, blazing past the screen door, where Rolex waited once more. The perfect feline didn't miss his opportunity to hiss at Special Agent Ryan.

Jane beelined for the bathroom and splashed cool water on her cheeks. That flush came from the Georgia heat, not the handsome officer of the law. She secured her fall of dark hair into a loose bun to cool off her neck, then took a little too long selecting the best hat to match her dress and guard against harmful UV rays. Decision, decisions.

At last, she settled on an adorable sun hat with purple stripes. After smoothing her bangs out of the way, she anchored the hat in place. Her lips twisted as she caught her reflection. Hmm. The headwear had looked adorable online but didn't quite compliment her features as she'd hoped. Oh well. Protection was protection, and adorable was adorable.

With a shrug, she retraced her steps, pausing at the door to talk to Rolex. "You behave, young man." He ignored her and growled at the agent. Yes, cats growled. The first time he'd done it, she'd feared a giant dog had followed him inside the house, determined to feast.

"Lose the hat," Fiona called from the doorway of the office.

Her friend had a bias against headwear, and Jane had no idea why. She pretended not to hear and slipped outside.

Special Agent Ryan canted his head to the side again, an interesting stance. "Nice, um, hat."

"Thank you," she said. See? Adorable. She bounded down the steps to take the lead. "This way." With a wave toward the house, in case Rolex or Fiona were watching her, she aimed for the cobblestone path, the Special Agent at her side. "So, the Garden of Memories is divided into six different sections, plus the mausoleum." Her usual spiel. "Autumn Grove is one of the oldest and the center of everything. Every other section offers easy access to it." She thought for a moment. "A smarter murderer would have chosen a gravesite on the outer edge of the cemetery for a quicker and easier escape, just in case things got dicey."

"Not if they were searching for something specific." He made a note on the map.

Ohhhh. Had the culprit chosen plot #39 for a reason? Rhonda Burgundy herself perhaps? "The section names are Eden Valley, Pleasant Green, Angel Wing, Serenity Rose, and Paradise Ladling. Oh, and the mausoleum. A hedgerow delineates each area which is connected by varying cobblestone paths. All but Paradise Ladling. That's my family plot. For the most part, it's isolated from the others." She pointed as she spoke, her heart clenching when she thought of Grandma Lily at rest. Jane visited her on the third Sunday of every month. Their special day.

"How large is the property?"

"We're up to seventy-five acres now. Over time, different Ladlings added to the grounds."

"That's a lot of land for one person to tend." He sounded impressed. "Any other staff?"

"There's no need. As Aurelian Hills grew into a bustling tourist attraction and hub for treasure hunters, our grounds became surrounded on all sides. Privately owned land to the north. An interactive mining camp to the south. A lake at the east, and undeveloped commercial property to the west. We are officially closed to new guests. Now burials are done at —" she worked her jaw— "Aurelian Hills Cemetery on the other side of town."

A corner of his mouth twitched. "Not a fan of Aurelian Hills Cemetery, are we?"

Did she detect a thread of laughter?

They rounded a sitting area—the Reflection Center— with benches shaded by the most magnificent wisteria trees with a wealth of gardenias in bloom around it.

"Do you receive many visitors out here?" he asked, returning to the business at hand.

"Someone comes out about once a week. Maybe twice. I also give a midnight tour of the grounds once a month, though attendance is sparse."

"Midnight tours. But no cameras." His tone had hardened again. "What security measures *do* you have in place?"

Ouch. His disapproval cut like a knife. "I have the gate up front and a brick wall around the acreage. Before you ask, I open the gate at sunup and close it at sundown. The hours depend on the season."

They turned a corner. "*You* close it?" he asked, that disapproval deepening. "Manually? Why?"

Cost, mostly. "Tradition." Also, not a lie. "My grandma would never forgive me if I installed an electric gate."

"Is she retired?"

Jane rested a hand over her aching heart. "No, she passed away three years ago. That's when I officially took over."

Actually, she'd taken over the year before, when Grandma Lily's health began to decline.

"I'm sorry for your loss."

"Thank you. I miss her so much, but at least I get to visit with her often. We just had tea last week, in fact." Moving on. "Anyway. I was raised here. I know the land and its residents better than I know the town's people."

"I get it," he said, projecting a new emotion. Understanding. "Trees and monuments never let you down, and the dead never leave." Then he cleared his throat, as if uncomfortable. "What's that building?" He pointed as they paused. They'd reached the end of the cobblestone path and the start of a gravel driveway. "It's not on the map."

Up ahead was a hill topped by the backside of a one-story version of the Victorian cottage. The white exterior had yellowed over time, the wood in need of serious repairs. Ivy grew over one side and encroached upon the roof.

"That's the official business office, such as it is, and what I wanted to show you. I removed it from the map because I'm never in it. But the original cobblestone path begins at the porch and leads to Autumn Grove. At night, this is the easiest track to follow, with the fewest twists, turns and skunks."

He made a notation. "Why don't you use the building?"

"Oh. That's where the ghosts live."

He missed a step, and she laughed.

"Teasing. Only teasing," she told him, and he huffed a breath. "I simply prefer the convenience of the cottage." The memories of working with her grandparents. "Plus, it isn't about to crumble into dust."

"Understandable." He stashed his notebook in his pocket. "If it's okay with you, I'd like to have a look around."

"Of course. Come on." She stepped forward, only to stop when he pivoted in front of her again, stopping her. "Yes? May I help you?" she asked, her heart thumping now. How did he resemble every romance-novel hero she'd ever read about? Even the paranormal ones. "Is there something else on your mind, Agent?"

"Please, call me Conrad," he suggested, and for some reason, she blushed.

Knowing she was blushing made her blush even harder. Argh! Thank goodness for the hat. The shade reduced her ridiculous reaction to a common courtesy.

Whoa, whoa, whoa. Had he just said his name was Conrad? She gulped. A drool-worthy man with a name that began with C. Her kryptonite.

They were going to date and break up, weren't they?

"I'm Jane. I mean, you already know my first name. But feel free to use it. Everyone else does. A few times, I've been called Jay Bird." Rambling again.

He pulled his gaze from her and scanned the area, saying, "Sheriff Moore mentioned you live out here alone."

Had he asked the sheriff about her? Well, duh. Of course, he had. *Suspect #1, remember?* "I'm not technically alone. I have Rolex."

"And he's terrifying, but he's not a genuine form of protection." The handsome agent rubbed the back of his neck, obviously feeling awkward. He'd lost both his sternness and his outer aura of charm. "I'd feel better knowing you had more security."

She would, too. "I'll look into hiring someone, I promise." It was called window shopping, and she did it often for a groundskeeper. Didn't mean she had to purchase anything.

When she attempted to move around him, he followed, blocking her.

"I'm sorry, Jane, but I'd like to view the property alone." He reached into his jacket pocket and handed her a business card. "If something new occurs or someone frightens you, call me. Also, you'll need to keep out of the

29

crime scene. We've sectioned it off. Do not bypass our tape. I'll be in touch if I have any other questions."

He walked away, not waiting for her response. Clearly, she'd been dismissed.

Jane pressed her tongue to the roof of her mouth and shook her head. See? The reason why dead people made better friends than living ones.

"Oh, one more thing, Miss Ladling." Special Agent— Conrad—paused his step to glance over his shoulder and slide his sunglasses into place. "Don't leave town."

CHAPTER THREE

Archie Dillion
Never Killed a Man That Didn't Need Killing.
Plot 54, Garden of Memories

"*D*on't leave town," Jane muttered as she and her hearse puttered along the road, catching the eye of anyone nearby. With a turn here and there, she passed the most expensive inn, the Manor at Prospect Street. A historic bed-and-breakfast and event room boasting Aurelian Hills's most luxurious rooms and finest dining experience.

One more turn, and she reached a gate blocking the wealthiest neighborhood from the rest of the town. Of course, the rest of the town knew the code, so...

The metal bars lifted, allowing Jane to enter. When she crested a hill, she spotted the first mansion. A sprawling estate made of white stone and tall glass, with a breathtaking manicured yard.

Any other time, she would have marveled at the luxurious design. Today, her mind whirled. Two days had passed. Two.

Days. Forty-eight endless hours. Had she received word from Conrad? Noooo. She'd even called and left him a message. And she was marginally certain she'd asked a question at some point during her two-minute ramble.

Bottom line: A murder had occurred in her backyard and the "special agent" couldn't bother to update her on the case? He was *so* not a romance-novel hero. Heroes broke curses. Or at least fought them. Heroes didn't ignore you at the most critical junctures of your life.

Fiona had one theory other than a jealous boyfriend or husband. They'd discussed it Friday night when they'd knitted at Jane's. Something they did every week. Her friend wondered if someone from the clinic did the deed. Rumors suggested some kind of fight had erupted among the staff the day before the murder.

The darling Fiona had provided more than information. She'd passed along the name of a new security expert in town. Someone willing to work cheap. Except the owner of Peach State Security had failed to return Jane's call too. Was she *that* forgettable?

Whatever! Onward and upward. Jane was taking matters into her own hands. If Conrad—Special Agent Ryan—considered her a suspect, fine. She would work to solve the murder and clear her good name. Bonus, she would end the besmirching of her family's legacy.

The absolute, utter jerkholes at Aurelian Hills Cemetery had begun a whisper campaign on the Headliner, claiming "guests" at Garden of Memories were no longer safe. That "underground home invasions" were rampant. Jane clenched her teeth.

An aluminum-foil-wrapped casserole was nestled on the passenger seat. No one could resist Jane's fried red-potato salad.

She parked in the circular driveway of the Hotchkinses,

noting the plethora of cars. Different models, colors and price tags, yet each one intimidated her. Oh, wow. Some of the vehicles were tagged with neon-blue spray paint. The same fleur-de-lys symbol covered hoods and doors. On purpose?

Focus. A quick internet search had revealed the number one suspect of any homicide: the spouse. So Jane's plan was simple. Lean on the age-old Southern tradition of bringing food to the bereaved in order to stealthily question Tiffany. *My first official interrogation.* Should be a piece of cake. Jane had spoken to lots of people in her life. Both dead and alive. Making words wasn't difficult.

Had there been trouble in paradise? Fiona called earlier this morning to mention some rumors.

A deep breath fortified Jane's courage. After swinging her purse over her shoulder, she grabbed the still-warm casserole dish and exited the hearse. A soft wind scented with hyacinths and azaleas rippled over the pretty black-and-white dress she'd found at Très Chic Consignment for a steal.

The home intimidated her more than the cars. Three stories of wealth and elegance.

On the wraparound porch, Jane checked to make sure she'd remembered her notebook. Excellent. She forced the corners of her mouth to lift. A comforting smile, probably. The one usually reserved for those who visited the Garden of Memories. She rang the bell.

To her surprise, Tiffany herself answered the door. Red-rimmed green eyes looked Jane over. The widow's tanned skin was now blotchy from tears, but not one strand of her dark bob dared move out of place. A skintight black dress hugged her perfect curves.

Am I looking at grief? Or guilt? Both?

Jane remembered the other woman as an effortless trend-setter who always knew the right thing to wear and say.

Based on the soft roar of conversation pouring from somewhere inside, guests packed the Hotchkins's home. The number of guests proved double or maybe triple the number of cars outside.

"Hello, Tiffany," she began with her best Garden of Memories smile. An expression that said, *I'm here to help. Everything will be okay.* "You might not remember me, but we attended Aurelian Hills High together. Go, Miners! Anyway. I'm Jane Ladling, and I'm so sorry about—"

"Another one?" Tiffany interjected, her tone both furious and overwrought. She glared down at the floor and stomped her foot. "You slept with Cemetery Girl, Marcus?"

Someone remembered Jane, at least. "I never slept with your husband. I barely even spoke to him. I just thought—"

"Whatever. It doesn't matter anyway." The scowling widow opened the door wider. "You might as well come in and join the others."

"I...thanks?" Jane's low heels clicked on the black-and-white marble as she entered the foyer. As her hostess led the way deeper into the home, she asked, "What happened to the cars?"

"What does it matter?"

Okay then. Her first interrogation had earned a solid F-so far.

The deeper she traveled, the louder the cacophony of voices became. Tiffany led her into a spacious sitting room overflowing with dozens of women. They lounged everywhere: the couch, the loveseat and even the uncomfortable-looking mahogany Queen Anne chairs someone must have dragged in from the formal dining room. Others stood here and there or leaned against the wall sipping a mimosa. A few guests openly cried.

Abandoning Jane, Tiffany shouldered through the sea of mourners. She poured and downed a drink at the wet bar in the corner. Then poured another. And another. With every gulp, more fury vibrated from her slight frame. The alcohol appeared to fuel fires of rage inside her.

A pretty, glassy-eyed brunette approached Jane. Someone she recognized from high school. An older woman who'd been a few years ahead. Abigail Waynes. No, Abigail Waynes-Kirkland now. "I'll show you where Tiffany keeps the casseroles, desserts and...whatever that is. The fridge is currently full, but we've set some ice chests."

Abigail didn't wait for Jane's response, just plowed forward, escorting her into the kitchen. Foil-wrapped dishes covered every available surface.

"Oh, wow, that's a lot of food." Available for the guests, too? Jane's mouth watered. She'd forgotten to eat breakfast.

"So," Abigail said, propping her hip against a counter and crossing her arms. "The good ole doc and the corpse collector. Did he give you his famous vitamin D injections in his exam rooms, too?"

What! In his exam rooms? "He never...I never...not with him, I swear!" With great effort, she managed to squeeze her culinary delight between what looked to be mango salsa and lasagna.

You're here to investigate. So investigate!

Jane nibbled on her bottom lip before asking, "Did *you* receive his, um, injections?"

The brunette gave her a *wouldn't you like to know* eye roll before sauntering off.

The answer was yes. Jane would very much like to know. Had Abigail slept with the doctor or not?

Before following the other woman, Jane jotted a handful of names found on cards next to some of the dishes and added a few observations in the trusty notebook.

Multiple confirmed affairs.

Spouse upset. Or faking.

Look into Abigail's romantic history. Is she on or off again with her husband? What causes their breakups?

Get recipe for mango salsa.

After retracing Abigail's steps, she returned to the lion's den. The alcohol had hit Tiffany with a vengeance.

She stumbled about, liquid splashing from the rim of her glass. "Did you not hear me?" she shrieked. "Anyone who slept with my husband can walk herself out of my house before I make her crawl out!"

The room erupted in a symphony of protests.

"I didn't! Only kissed him a little. But so did Stacey!"

"I would never! Not again."

"Don't look at me. I told Tiff he was only using her for her money and she should kick him out. And not so I could snatch him up!"

Women glanced around the room, some glaring daggers, others trying to blend into the background. Jane casually added another handful of names to her notebook. If her list of suspects kept growing like this, she'd soon need another notebook. Or several dozen of them. If she didn't know a name, she described the face.

One spectator's reaction intrigued her more than any other. That of Emma Miller. A pretty nurse with a slender build and hair too light to be brown but too dark to be blonde. Jane recognized her from the clinic website. Emma worked with Dr. Hotchkins, so she wasn't someone Jane had dealt with. Dr. Garcia worked one side of the office, and Dr. Hotchkins had worked the other.

Cheeks red, eyes wide, Emma hurried from the room. Hmm. An action born of guilt or a need to escape the fireworks?

Jane gave chase. Too late. From the porch, Jane watched as a sobbing Emma sped down the driveway.

Drats! Well, no matter. Jane would call and make an

appointment at the clinic. Wasn't like Emma could avoid her there.

With a sigh, Jane decided to return home rather than rejoin the party. Er, wake. She slid into the hearse, but she didn't hurry off. Once again, the fleur-de-lys symbols caught her attention. Had the five cars been vandalized or had the girls hired an artist? Was this connected to the case? Or was she grasping at straws?

Better safe than sorry. Jane exited and logged the license plate numbers of the tagged vehicles before heading home. Rolex greeted her from the living room couch. After offering him the requisite snuggles, she got to work, walking the grounds to shoo away any lookie-loos hoping to catch a glimpse of the murder site. Outside of a holiday and a tour, the cemetery rarely received more than three guests. Today, that number was doubled.

When she returned to the cottage, she stopped by the kitchen for a drink of water and caught sight of Special Agent Ryan's business card, resting beneath an apple magnet on the fridge.

Why not call him and share what she'd learned?

Yes, why not, Jane? Investigators solve more crimes when they share information.

Unable to conjure a good reason not to share, she dug her cell phone from the pocket of her dress. For some reason, her fingers tingled as she dialed his number.

He answered on the second ring. "Special Agent Ryan."

His deep, husky voice sent shivers down her spine. "Hi. Hello. I was calling to see if you've interviewed Tiffany Hotchkins. The wife." Jane flipped through her notebook. "Tiffany is certain her husband had an affair with tons of locals. Abigail Waynes-Kirkland might or might not have been one of those women. Apparently, Dr. Hotchkins gave, um, *vitamin D* injections in exam rooms. Um...you know what that means, right? Anyway, most of the women are single, but some are married. You'll want to look into their spouses too probably. I have a list of names and descriptions."

"Jane Ladling?" he asked with a tinge of amusement.

Heat filled her cheeks, quickly spreading through the rest of her. *Focus.* "Right. Sorry. Yes, this is Jane Ladling. Why don't I start over?" Deep breath in. "Have you interviewed Dr. Hotchkins's wife? Or her friend, Abigail Waynes-Kirkland?"

The agent's sigh crackled over the line. "I'm currently pursuing several people of interest. That's all I can tell you."

Several? *Don't ask. Don't you dare.* "Am I still one of those people?" Argh! She'd asked.

A pause. Then, "There's definite interest in you here at the bureau, Jane."

Wait. What? His words had a flirtatious edge—and so did his tone. She caught herself doodling *Mrs. Special Agent Conrad Ryan* and drawing hearts.

Focus! Was she or wasn't she in trouble here? "There's something else you should know," she told him, forging ahead. "Dr. Hotchkins's nurse may or may not be one of the women who may or may not have had an affair with him. I'm not sure yet."

"Yet?" Another sigh, this one heavier. "Do not question anyone or look into the case, Jane. That's my job. Do you understand?"

Equally unwilling to lie or give up, she bypassed the question entirely. "Look, you missed a wild scene at the Hotchkins's house this morning. Tiffany accused everyone of sleeping with her husband. Emma Miller, his nurse, rushed out crying and sped away. I've even heard Dr. Hotchkins argued with his staff the day before his murder. Don't you find that the tiniest bit suspicious?"

"What I find suspicious is your visit to the widow of the victim found on your property. A man you claim you've never spoken with. Why would you do that?"

"Because it's polite. I didn't know the doctor, but I went to high school with Tiffany." Rolex wove through her legs and meowed for a second breakfast. "Someone has to solve the crime, put a murderer away, and clear the good names of the innocent."

"That's right. Someone has to, and it's me. Trust me on this. I'm working as fast as humanly possible."

The fierce promise underlying his statement comforted and delighted her. But it wouldn't stop her. "Everyone needs help now and then, and you could clearly use mine. You wouldn't have this lead about Dr. Hot's nurse without me. You're welcome, by the way."

"I'm going to pretend I didn't hear you call him by that ridiculous nickname. And I've been looking into the clinic employees since day one." He said no more.

"Well? Have you found anything?"

Sigh. "I'm pursuing several people of interest," he repeated. The sound of papers rustling drifted to her ear. "Did you get someone out there to beef up security?"

Using her shoulder to anchor her phone in place, Jane picked up Rolex and carried him to the couch. "I called a local business from..." What was the name of the company? Oh yes. "Peach State Security. We haven't managed to connect. Apparently he just opened up shop, so I'm going to give him a couple more days."

"I instructed Sheriff Moore to have a deputy patrol the cemetery each night, but he doesn't have the resources to spare the man much longer. Nor do I. If you don't hear back from Peach State Security by the end of business today, let me know. I'm acquainted with several firefighters here in Atlanta who install security equipment on their off days."

"Okay, will do," she said, trying not to melt into a boneless heap. Other than her grandparents and Fiona, no one had ever worried about her wellbeing. Not that anyone wanted her to die. Not that anyone in Aurelian Hills hated her. She was just…overlooked.

When a loud knock echoed through the house, scaring Rolex, Jane closed her notebook and popped to her feet. "Gotta go. I've got a visitor. No doubt it's someone else wanting a look at the crime scene. Don't worry, though. Rolex and I are taking care of it." She disconnected before he had a chance to do more than sputter. Oops.

She rushed to the open door, a tower of strength suddenly standing before her. A white T-shirt hugged sculpted muscle. Denims and combat boots showcased a body built like a Mack Truck.

A familiar face kick-started her heart, and a bright smile bloomed. "Beau?"

He nodded without returning her smile. "That's me."

Beauregard "Beau" Harden. *This* was the nice young man Fiona had mentioned? The one who'd just returned to town?

Wow! The shy boy had grown into a gorgeous man. He was taller than she remembered, but he possessed the same thick pale waves and green eyes. Once warm, those stunning irises now appeared ice cold. A scar bisected one of his brows.

"Hello Jane," he said, a little gruff. Not quite the soft, eager voice she recalled from school.

He remembered her. How wonderful. "Hello, Beau. It's so nice to see you again."

"You called about security." He rocked back on his heels. "I thought I'd visit rather than call."

"I'm so glad you did." Beau had joined the navy right after commencement, leaving Aurelian Hills in his rear-view, but she'd never forgotten him. As children, the tow-headed kid had always offered her encouragement. He'd eaten every lunch at her side, and he'd never abandoned her on the playground, even when other kids teased him about being buried alive by the Cemetery Girl.

When no one had asked her to dance during their senior graduation party, he'd taken her in his arms and swayed. Jane had never forgotten his kindness.

He lifted a brow. "You going to invite me in?"

"Oh! Yes, yes, of course. Please, come in, Beau," she said, stepping aside.

He wiped his boots on the welcome mat and entered the cottage far too small for his broad shoulders.

"Have a seat anywhere you'd like." Wait. "Where are my manners? Are you thirsty?" She hurried to the kitchen before he could respond and poured two sweet teas. Rolex watched from the table. By the time she returned to the living room, Beau had chosen the recliner next to the couch.

Rolex followed her and jumped on his lap, gazing with adoration, as if he wanted Beau to pet him. A total psych-out. As soon as her childhood friend reached, Rolex hissed, scratched and darted off. His signature move. Two round punctures topped two bleeding lines on Beau's hand, set in a zigzag pattern.

He winced but didn't complain or even tense, making Jane beam as she handed over his drink, then settled across from him.

He eyed her with unwavering focus. "Tell me what you need from me."

No more pleasantries? No catching up? No warmth? Forget the Mack Truck; he was an iceberg.

Was he married? Did he have children? So many of their classmates did. Or was he single?

Good gracious. Fiona was the one who'd given Jane the

card. Which meant she had set this up as a re-meet cute. Meet cute on repeat?

Reeling, she placed her glass on the coffee table and patted her lap twice. Rolex jumped up and glared at Beau. "I don't know what you've heard, but there was a disturbance out here a few nights ago. A murder. When the agent from the GBH realized I didn't have any security cameras, or any form of security at all, he suggested I contact a professional immediately."

"You have no security whatsoever?" Beau scanned the room, as if cataloging millions of access points available to every criminal in town. And out. Concern etched his harsh features. "He was right."

He? He who? "Here's the thing. My budget is very limited." Understatement of the year. She lived on the cemetery's trust.

He didn't miss a beat. He simply nodded, as if her lack of funds were no big deal. "I'm sure we can work something out. I'll feel better knowing you have protection out here."

Similar to what Conrad had said. Er, Special Agent Ryan. Or better yet, Agent Spice. Had anyone ever smelled so good? "What do you suggest I get?"

Leaning toward her, he braced his elbows on his knees. The scent of pine and soap wafted to her nose. And something else. A softer note she couldn't quite place. She frowned. A flower of some sort? So different from Conrad but just as pleasant.

"You need a better lock on the front door," he said. "Also, a motion detector near every window. To start."

The air seeped from her lungs. "Anything else?" she squeaked. He might as well have listed the moon. No way she could afford that stuff, even if they "worked something out." Whatever that meant.

"I'll need to inspect the grounds to get a better idea."

Of course, he would. "Let me grab a hat, and I'll show you around."

Finally, his expression softened, a hint of his old smile teasing his mouth. "You still collect hats?"

"Everyone needs a hobby," she said, standing with Rolex in her arms.

"Did you ever find the perfect fit?"

"Not yet. But it's only a matter of time." She winked and strolled off with a lighter step than before. "Rolex, my love," she muttered, setting him down inside her bedroom. "My friend is back in town, and he's here to help us. Things are looking up. Surely!"

CHAPTER FOUR

Samuel Lee
Taking My Secrets with Me.
Plot 153, Garden of Memories

Things were absolutely *not* looking up.

After the tour—which did not involve the friendly chit chat she'd anticipated—Beau zoomed off to gather the necessary supplies, with a promise to return on Monday. But Monday came and went, and he never showed. And yes, he'd said, "Monday. Probably." Still! A call wouldn't be amiss.

Special Agent Ryan hadn't called, either, so he didn't know she was continuing her investigation. That she'd scheduled an appointment with Dr. Garcia on Tuesday. Mr. Special Agent didn't know the fleur-de-lys had become a thorn in her brain, constantly pricking her thoughts. What did it mean to the person who'd painted it? And why hadn't the agent called her? Had the Ladling curse mutated and strengthened and now affected *every* relationship, big and small, romantic and nonromantic?

Maybe fate expected her to spend the rest of her life in flux, always expecting the worst. A cosmic punishment for a crime committed by her ancestor. And she wasn't being dramatic about this. Nope. She only reacted to the circumstances forced upon her.

Just as she exited the shower on the morning of her appointment, the Aurelian Hills Medical Clinic number popped up on her cell phone. Hmm. They'd never called her before an appointment before. Had Emma seen Jane's name on the schedule and raised an alarm? Did the entire staff suspect her of wrongdoing? Of being well and seeking answers?

"Hello?" she said, hesitant.

"I'm calling for Jane Ladling."

"I am she. I mean, me. I am me. I mean, I'm Jane." Goodness gracious. *Get yourself together!*

"Hi, Jane." The soft, feminine voice developed a friendly pitch. "This is Caroline Whittington, Dr. Garcia's physician's assistant here at the medical center. I'm sorry to call so early, but this couldn't wait."

"No problem." PA Caroline Whittington. An employee Jane had never met. Was this a scam, then? A way to gain access to her medical records? Although she hadn't visited the clinic in more than a year, so updating was probably necessary. Jane decided to test her. "So good to hear from you again."

"Again? Please, forgive me but I don't recall speaking to you before this."

Okay. That tracked. Wait. Her cemetery training kicked in. *Always start with kindness.* "How may I help you?"

"I'm afraid Dr. Garcia is unable to see you today. Yesterday evening someone spray-painted the clinic, as well as our vehicles. He's involved in clean-up."

"Spray paint, you say." Her back went ramrod straight. "Tell me everything. The color. The image or words."

"Oh. Um. The perpetrator drew a fleur-de-lys. Blue, I think. Or maybe green."

Fleur-de-lys again. Most likely blue. Prick, prick, prick. Gah! Why did this matter? Was there something here or not? "Do you know who did it? Or maybe you have a suspect? A clue? Do you know *why* they did it?"

"No suspects or clues." A pause. "Do *you* know who did it or why?"

Uh-oh. From sweet tone to accusatory, as if Jane hoped to cover her own tracks. "I noticed the same symbol spray-painted on other cars and got curious." Truth.

The response must have pacified the other woman. Tone softer, she said, "My apologies for snapping at you. As you can imagine, this is a tough time. Someone in town is targeting random people, marking buildings and cars with a ridiculous lily flower, doing thousands of dollars in damage. And to what purpose? Why hurt those of us mourning the loss of Dr. Hotchkins?" A choking sound clogged the line, as if the assistant was fighting tears.

Sympathy churned in Jane's stomach. "I'm so sorry for your loss." Forget the investigation for a moment. Loss hurt. This PA had clearly cared about her coworker. But maybe a wee bit too much? Had they been friends or something more?

Okay, so, Jane wasn't forgetting the investigation anytime soon.

"Thank you. The entire town feels the sting of this one, I'm sure." Caroline sniffled, then cleared her throat. "Did you know him?"

Know, as in the biblical sense? "I know his wife." *Did* you know *him?* Jane went ahead and etched Caroline Whittington into her mental list of suspects.

"A lovely woman. How devastated she must be." Silence stretched for a moment as Caroline seemed to collect herself. "Now then. The reason I called. If you are amenable, I'm happy to see you at the scheduled time."

"I am amenable, yes. I'll be there." Emma aided both Dr. Hotchkins and the PA. Two birds, one stone. "I appreciate your willingness to see me last minute, Caroline."

"My pleasure. I'll see you at ten, Miss Ladling."

Oops. They weren't on a first name basis? "Can't wait." And she couldn't. At first. Jane enjoyed low-grade anticipation most of the morning. By the time she reached the clinic, however, she was battling a nervous stomach. What ailment brought her to see the good doctor? What wouldn't require a needle? And what questions should she ask Emma? Not to mention new suspect Caroline?

A handful of cars occupied the parking lot, with a single work truck idling at the curb near the front door. An older man was scrubbing the wall, where half of a neon-blue fleur-de-lys stained the white brick. Yep. Crafted by the same artist who'd vandalized the cars at Tiffany's.

Why would someone start this after the murder? Why start this at all? Why target Dr. Hotchkins's coworkers? What did anyone stand to gain from it?

Jane parked and made her way inside the building. After signing in, she claimed a seat in the back and set up camp. Minutes passed. She tapped a pen against the arm of her chair, her trusty notebook in hand. The internet had provided the top two motives for any crime: love or money. Had the handsome doctor and his nurse—and/or physician assistant—engaged in a love affair gone wrong? Maybe the doctor had promised to leave his wife and then balked?

What about money? And the other possibilities? Perhaps the doctor had argued with Emma over her role in the medical practice. A reason for the fight among the staff? Had she demanded compensation? Maybe he'd caught Caroline making a medical mistake or stealing pills.

What if Jane totally missed the mark here? Some people committed unspeakable acts just for grins and giggles. Or street cred. Street cred was still a thing, right?

A hoarse, hacking cough boomed. Two other patients waited with her. Both had glassy eyes and red noses. They sneezed again and again and again and again and again. One of them repeatedly lumbered past her to remind the receptionist that he was dying. What a baby.

"Miss Ladling?" called a nurse in bright scrubs with colorful butterflies. Emma!

Jane jolted out of the chair, her stomach twisting anew. "Present! I mean, I'm here. That's me. I'm Miss Ladling. Jane." Sweat glazed her palms as she haphazardly stuffed her notebook in her purse. "I mean, I know you know who I am. We've met before. Once. Kind of. We were in the same location, but we didn't chat or anything. Not that it wouldn't have been great to chat with you outside of an appointment." Well, she'd finally found the perfect ailment for today's visit. Diarrhea of the mouth. "Yikes. Sorry."

Emma offered a forced smile. "It's okay. People can get really worked up when they're not feeling well, and they're worried about the underlying cause." Like Caroline, she mourned Dr. Hotchkins. Or the strain of hiding his murder was taking a toll.

Suspecting everyone I meet of the crime? This is my life now?

Well. Why stop? Jane zeroed in on the golden band around Emma's finger. A wedding ring. *The plot thickens.* Would the nurse kill a man to hide an affair or maybe even spark drama with her husband?

"Come on back," Emma said. "We're ready for you in room two."

"Wonderful." As both the sickies glared at her, she kicked

into motion, closing the distance and breezing past the door between the waiting room and hallway of patient rooms.

After taking Jane's weight, Emma ushered her into the right exam room. Same sterile beige walls as usual, one of which was covered in framed certificates. A tiled floor and a ceiling with slight water stains.

"I see you have a pet," Emma said, grabbing the blood pressure cuff. "A dog? Big? Small?"

"A cat, actually. Rolex. He's the brightest light of my life." Jane sat on the examination table and settled her purse at her side. "But, uh, how did you see that I had a pet?" Like with a psychic vision or something?

"The fur on your dress."

Oh yes. That made more sense.

"Is Rolex friendly or one of those demon spawns?" Emotionless, the nurse secured the cuff on Jane's arm.

"Oh, my Rolex is a perfect angel." No truer statement had ever been spoken.

"I have a corgi named Cheddar, and he seems to shed an entire fur coat every day. I don't care, though, because I love him so much."

Heartfelt words delivered with such a deadened tone. Highly suspicious? No longer. Right? Anyone with a dog named Cheddar *couldn't* be a murderer. It was practically science. Maybe Emma's coldness showcased a woman fighting to hold herself together over the death of a friend. Or lover.

Staring at the table, she pumped a balloon and the cuff filled with air. Avoiding eye contact with a patient? Standard procedure or the action of a guilty woman?

A frown tugged at the corners of Emma's mouth, slowly deepening. Was something wrong?

Jane followed her gaze to the open purse at her side, with a page of the notepad visible. Heat singed her cheeks. Had

Emma spotted the ridiculous hearts Jane had drawn around Conrad's name?

"Ow!" The cuff squeezed far too tight, pain shooting to her shoulder.

"Sorry, sorry," Emma rushed out, jolting into focus. The pressure on her bicep eased.

Okay. Let's get back on track. Emma might be the first bad guy to own a dog named Cheddar. Her (seeming) recognition of Conrad's name—no big deal. For all Jane knew, the special agent had interviewed the clinic's employees at length. But why react so strongly to Jane's obvious schoolgirl crush? Unless the nurse had been lost in her thoughts? Like Jane was now?

She shook her head to focus. One interrogation, coming up. She would start off easy, then go in for the kill. Metaphorically speaking. "Does Cheddar mind strangers? Because Rolex hates everyone with the heat of a thousand suns. Especially the GBH agents running around my place because of…you know. Dr. Hotchkins. The murderer."

The color in Emma's cheeks drained, and she took a deep breath to steady herself. "Yes, that must have been quite the shock to you both." With an audible swallow, she hooked her stethoscope over her neck and freed Jane from the cuff.

"It was, yes, but I'm sure things are worse for you. You knew the doctor personally." Oh man. Where were her manners? "I'm so sorry for your loss," she rushed to add.

Emma nodded in acknowledgement but offered nothing else on the subject. "Your blood pressure is one twenty-nine over eighty." Her flat tone was back.

"Is that, uh, bad or something?"

"It's slightly elevated." She replaced the device on its hook and typed Jane's results into a note-taking tablet. "Most likely due to stress."

"Yes, most likely." Jane wasn't ready to let the subject

drop. "Poor Dr. Hotchkins. He's the reason my stress is so high. I just can't get him off my mind." Truth.

Had the other woman flinched?

"He's definitely missed." An even flatter tone. "I need silence for this next test, okay?" Emma aimed the temperature gauge at her forehead.

Silence? For a thermometer? Definitely a lie.

"No fever," Emma said. "So what brings you in here today?"

Murder. If the nurse thought she'd successfully changed the subject, she thought wrong. "I'm here because of Dr. Hotchkins. You know, my stress. The upset of it all. I'm the one who found his body." Yes. The perfect excuse. It had a foundation of truth and left the door open for further questions. "My heart has raced at odd times." Whenever a certain special agent neared. "I toss and turn at night." Dreaming of said special agent. "Flutters erupt in my belly."

This time, Emma definitely flinched. "I did hear about your involvement in the case." After making a few more notes in the device, she headed to the door. "The PA will be in shortly." With that, she exited, sealing Jane inside the room, alone, unable to blurt out her next query.

Her abruptness proved startling. Well. That was *definitely* suspicious. Jane opened her notebook to draw stars around Emma's name.

With nothing to do but wait, she scanned the quintessential sickroom, taking in other details. Standard exam table with a paper cover. A row of glass containers displayed cotton balls, long swabs and tongue depressors. On the wall hung a biohazard disposal container for needles. Jane shuddered and looked away.

Here and there, medical posters listed symptoms for various diseases. She examined the certificates more closely.

A framed PA diploma for Caroline Whittington, as well as different awards.

A clipped knock sounded, and Caroline entered the room, peering down at the same iPad Emma had used. The door closed behind her.

At the sink, she washed her hands. "Hello, Miss Ladling." Her perfunctory manner seemed at odds with her show of emotion over the phone. What had changed? The thirty-something PA had red hair and pale, freckled skin. Unlike Emma, she wore plain blue scrubs. Gaze direct and unwavering, she offered Jane a swift smile. "Nice to put a face with a voice. Your file says you're upset about finding Dr. Hotchkins's body. But I must be honest with you. You didn't seem upset when we spoke on the phone."

She suspects me of lying. Because she was an accurate judge of truth, or because she was guilty of lying herself? "Everyone deals with grief differently." Truth.

"Well. You aren't wrong." The woman's features fell, her shoulders rolling in, as if she were too exhausted to hide her emotions a moment longer. She massaged her temples. "I'm sorry. This has just been *a day*."

"Oh. Um. Of course. Certainly." An abrupt change. *Too* abrupt?

"It must have been awful for you," Caroline said, reaching out to pat her shoulder. Too understanding and sympathetic? Or a normal amount?

Jane didn't know anything anymore. "It *really* was," she replied in earnest. All those cars on her driveway, some on her lawn. Booted feet trampling everywhere.

The PA eased onto a stool beside the exam table, her expression much softer. "Tell me how I can help you, Jane. Are you having trouble sleeping?"

"Yes!" Ugh. She hadn't meant to shout her response, but as mentioned before, she'd only tossed and turned last night, lost in thoughts about Conrad. He was single, but was he interested in Jane? Did she want him to be? The curse... "I probably shouldn't have come here." A statement the agent would agree with, no doubt. "I mean, you guys know—knew —and loved Dr. Hotchkins. Everyone at the clinic must be as upset as I am. More so."

Let the investigation continue!

A hint of sadness clung to Caroline. "First, you should always seek help if you need it, Jane. Never hesitate. Second, yes, Dr. Hotchkins is certainly missed. He was an amazing man who often volunteered his time at a free medical facility in the city."

"Oh, how wonderful." She hesitated for only a moment before adding, "Do you happen to know the name of the facility? So I can make a donation in Dr. Hotchkins's honor." And maybe, possibly, stop by and offer her deepest sympathies. Chat. Couldn't hurt, right?

Blink, blink. "I'm sorry, I don't know offhand. But I can certainly find out."

"No worries." No reason to give the woman one more thing to do. Jane made a mental note to do a little research herself. A way to bone up her skills.

Caroline patted her hand and sighed. "I'm going to prescribe something to help you rest and refer you to a therapist I know. Someone who specializes in this kind of trauma. Now." She motioned to Jane's arm. "Let's talk about that cut."

The scratch she'd gotten when she'd gardened this morning? "That? It's no big deal. I get all kinds of scrapes working at the cemetery." As the lone employee, she did all the gardening and repairs herself.

"All kinds of scrapes, yet you're overdue for a tetanus vaccination. I'd rather not treat you for a toxic bacterium later on. While I get your prescription sent to the pharmacy and draft up your referral, Nurse Emma will take care of the injection."

What? "No! No needles. I'm fine. Honest. Better than fine. Really! I made everything up. I'm not really upset about finding a dead body." Nervous laugh. "I've already forgotten it."

"Don't worry." Again, she patted Jane's hand. "We'll have you feeling better in no time."

JANE GRUMBLED as she stalked out of the clinic—and plowed straight into a grumbling Dr. Garcia. They stumbled apart, both going quiet. His eyes widened before he darted his gaze elsewhere.

"What are you doing here?" he growled. He was a short, rotund man with dark skin and darker eyes. "You shouldn't be here."

"Oh." Should none of his patients be here, or Jane specifically? "I rescheduled with the PA." Did no one tell him? Hmm.

Whatever. She would dissect the nuances of this interaction later and seize the opportunity being offered to her now. "Hey. While I've got you. I'd like to express my condolences for your great loss and to also offer to help you solve the mystery of the fleur-de-lys symbol and avenge the destruction of your property." Thoughts came, escaping her mouth before she had time to check them. "Has anyone ever visited you or Dr. Hotchkins with symptoms of, I don't know, artist's elbow? That's a thing, yes? Or maybe you have a patient who was once wearing a speck of neon-blue paint?"

"I can't discuss my patients with you, Miss Ladling." He hurried on as if his feet were on fire, entering the building.

Well. That was all kinds of wrong. And okay, yes, she

might be getting a bit paranoid here. But come on! The killer probably knew Jane owned and operated the cemetery. Which meant anyone acting weird toward her was potentially hiding something. One hundred percent. No question. This encounter with Dr. Garcia topped the list of weird.

She pondered his motives while driving home, her arm stinging from the totally unnecessary shot she'd been unable to avoid. She was only slightly massively more confused about Dr. Hotchkins's murder. During the course of her investigation, her list of suspects had only grown. So far she had crossed out a grand total of zero names.

Emma Miller and Tiffany Hotchkins still topped the list. Along with Caroline Whittington and Dr. Garcia, the receptionist at the clinic and both guys with colds. They couldn't have been as sick as they'd pretended to be, making her wonder if they acted worse as some kind of cover. Oh, also on her list were all the guests at Tiffany's house, plus everyone's significant other.

When she came to an active railroad crossing, getting stuck in a line of waiting cars, she phoned Fiona to tell all. "Do you know anything about these people?"

"Emma Miller. Let's see, let's see," Fiona said. "Oh, yes. I remember reading about Emma and her husband on the Headliner. They've been on the rocks for months. In fact, I think they're the ones who had a tiff at the Golden Spoon. She accused him of being an absentee husband, and he called her a cheating witch. But with a B." She spoke the last with a scandalized tone. "As for Caroline, I ran into her at the Yellow Brick Abode Library. By accident, I happened to notice she was checking out a stack of books about the art of flirting. If you know what I mean."

Interesting. Emma had (allegedly) engaged in an extramarital affair, and her husband had known about it.

Time for Jane to do a deep dive on the town app.

"Do you happen to remember the title of those books?" she asked. "For the case, I mean." Not for Conrad or anything like that.

A horn blasted, and Jane jolted. The train had moved on and so had the cars in front of her.

"Gotta go," she blurted out. "I'll call you in a bit. In the meantime, be thinking about that book title. For the case. Love you, bye." She hung up and motored on, entering her neighborhood only ten minutes later.

Ugh. An unfamiliar truck was parked outside her cottage. More lookie-loos in need of shooing? Wait. Bold letters decorated the old, beat-up truck. Peach State Security. She grinned, her bad day suddenly looking up. Beau had returned.

She rushed out of the hearse and to his truck. Huh. He wasn't in the cab. But he wasn't nearby either. Not that she could see. Where had he gone?

Hammering noises drew her to the side of the cottage. A ladder was propped against the wall, a shirtless and sweaty Beau in the middle of it.

She marveled at how much he both did and didn't resemble the little boy he'd once been. One thing was certain: the Beau of her memories hadn't packed so many muscles. Denim hung low on his waist, revealing the upper band of his underwear. Black briefs, if she had to venture a guess.

He climbed down and approached, towering over her. "You're back."

"And you're here," she said, confused. "Working."

He rubbed the back of his neck before motioning to a spot on the ground, where tools and all kinds of things she couldn't identify were piled. "I brought the equipment you needed and thought I'd get started."

Without going over a list with her? *Do not faint.* "I mean

this in the best possible way, but, um, everything looks so expensive."

"The manufacturers of the cameras, glass-break detectors, door and window sensors, and motion sensors gave them to me as a promotional tool, so you don't owe me a thing."

Oh, thank goodness! "I'll still compensate you for the labor, though," she pointed out.

He averted his gaze. "Tell you what, you put a Protected by Peach State Security sign at the gate, and we'll call it good."

The frugal side of her wanted to shout *yes!* "While I'm happy to display your sign, I'm not happy to take advantage of your time and efforts. I insist on paying your usual fee, but I can only spare two hundred dollars. What will that get me?" If she ate cheap noodles and peanut butter sandwiches for the rest of her life, she could pay him with her food budget. Maybe Beau would convince Fiona to feed Jane blueberry pancakes soon.

"Look," he said and sighed. "There's no advantage taking if I'm offering. So, how about this? I'll work for a few hours today and install as much as I can. If I need to come back, I'll send you a bill." He wiped his brow with a blue-and-white bandana. "Since you're home, I'll mount the cameras throughout the cemetery. That way, you and your demon spawn won't have to listen to my hammer. I know I can't enter the crime scene, but I'd like to position one camera near it."

"Perfect. I'll grab a hat and show you the way. Oh, and Rolex is a saint."

"No need to escort me," he said with no hint of emotion. "I remember the correct path."

Man, she missed the sweet, shy boy from before. And, okay, yeah, there'd been hints of this aloofness even then. But not with her. Never her. He'd always had smiles for little Jane. What charm did adult Jane lack? "Glad you remember the way, but I'm still escorting you. You're officially my favorite person right now, so I'm giving you the VIP treatment. Just give me five minutes." See? Charming.

She rushed inside, offered Rolex his required attention, and selected the best sunhat for her current dress. Another fit and flare, pink with white polka dots. Then, back out she went. On the porch, she grabbed a dog treat from the metal container next to Fiona's rocking chair.

"I'm ready," Jane called, bounding down the steps and joining him.

Beau noticed the treat and arched his brow. "You have a dog?"

"Kind of. Come on, and I'll introduce you to him. I think you'll become fast friends."

They walked the required trail side by side, comfortably silent. A tool belt now circled his waist, but he'd donned a plain white T-shirt, no skin—or underwear—visible. He carried a black duffel over his shoulder, filled with some of the equipment no doubt.

Surely some girl had locked this man down, and this wasn't a setup arranged by Fiona. As handsome as he was, Jane's thoughts continued to return to Conrad.

When would he call?

"You're probably wondering if I've ever seen a ghost out here," Jane said, not so comfortable anymore. "I haven't. My grandmother used to call me anti-paranormal. One of the reasons I'm such a good fit here, I guess. I haven't even heard the cries of the departed the way she did. Anyway, about the dog. We're crossing into the Garden's oldest section. There's a tradition, you see. When a new cemetery opens, the first occupant becomes a recently passed dog to keep guard over the bodies and allow the souls to pass in peace. As a little girl,

I came up with my own ritual. Only my favorite people get to meet the Garden's first resident, Muffin."

"That's…"

Trying to find a nice way to say "creepy"?

"Pretty wonderful," he finished, and she beamed at him.

They reached Muffin's headstone. The most elaborate marker in the entire cemetery, with a life-size metal sculpture of a golden retriever surrounded by equally life-size metal toys, welded to a thick base. A ball, a bone, and a shoe. Her steps faltered as she realized there was a new toy in the mix. One that blended perfectly. Was that a…crowbar?

Frowning, she leaned closer. Definitely a crowbar. Dirt smeared the sides, some specks darker than others…with a red tint?

Jane gasped as realization punched her. "Oh, my goodness!"

"What? What's wrong?" Beau darted his gaze, as if searching for a bad guy to demolish. His entire body vibrated with tension as he balled his hands into fists. "Did you see someone?"

"I think we just discovered the murder weapon."

CHAPTER FIVE

Dr. Gabriel Dansing
Forever Out of the Office.
Plot 1205, Garden of Memories

"*T*hat man is like a fine wine, only getting better with age." Fiona sat in her rocking chair before the unlit hearth, knitting.

Jane grinned as she worked a string of yarn through the first cast-on stitch. For the past half hour, she'd worked beside Fiona, knitting as well. They'd chatted about old times and laughed. Then Sheriff Moore had shown up unannounced to guard the (possible) murder weapon until Conrad's arrival. Fiona had spoken of little else since.

A common enough occurrence. This time was different because Jane had caught herself doing the same thing—with Conrad.

Something warm settled in her chest at the thought of seeing the special agent again.

Was he half as eager to see her? A third as eager? Even the merest scooch?

As she threaded a second stitch, she slid her gaze to the couch. How would Rolex react? Her precious kitty was currently posted on the top cushion behind Beau, swiping at him anytime he leaned back. Which he did. Often. He reclined with her laptop balanced on a pillow as he inspected camera connections. His features remained blank, yet tension seeped from him.

If he didn't have a girlfriend, he needed one. Someone who would help him relax. While Jane couldn't enjoy a happily ever after of her own, she wholeheartedly believed other people should experience theirs.

"Speaking of fine wine," she announced. "Do you have a girlfriend, Beau?" Why not get this conversation going? If Fiona hoped to set them up, the truth needed to come out. Jane and Beau could laugh and move on from there. Then Jane could take over match making duties for him. The thought excited her. Another adventure! Finally, she understood the appeal for Fiona.

What did he wish for in a girl? What did *Conrad* want? Confidence? Drive? A femme fatale? Quirkiness? A tendency to ramble? A collection of hats?

"No girlfriend," Beau replied, giving her a look that said, *I know what you're doing.*

"But you've had one? Long term? Or maybe more than one?"

"Yes. One long term. And I don't want another one. Relationships aren't a good fit for me."

Jane pursed her lips—*caught red-handed!* She gazed at Fiona for help.

The pancake-baking genius hurried to stop a laugh and glanced down at her knitting. Translation: *You run this interrogation on your own.*

Very well. She would! "Let's say relationships are a *wonderful* fit for you. Describe your perfect girl," she said to

Beau. "What are you looking for in a forever mate?"

"I'm not looking."

"Why not?" She was being nosy, but she didn't care. How else would she learn what she needed to know?

Fiona gaped at her, all *who are you and when did you get this bold?*

"I'm not discussing this with you," he grumbled.

Too bad, so sad. "Well, guess what? I *am* discussing it with you. What if we internet dated together? We can pick each other's dates." A small sacrifice on her part to reach a desired end—Beau's happiness. "We should at least download the same app and compare notes." It wasn't the worst idea she'd ever had.

A little dating might do her some good, too. Since her heart was locked in a coffin and buried too deep to find, she wouldn't have to worry about any breaks. She could get to know new people. Laugh, maybe. Finally, she would stop thinking of Special Agent Conrad Ryan and his wild effect on her.

"If I want a date, I'll get myself a date." His tone said: *Bring this up again, and I'm gone.*

"Oh, very well." Jane knew when to surrender. "I'll internet date all on my own." She paused her knitting long enough to do a search on her phone. And yes, to tease him a little. "This app looks promising. Smash at First Sight."

His tension intensified as he flipped up his gaze, focusing on her. "I'll download a dating app with you, but not that one. I get to choose."

"Deal," she shouted before he changed his mind. As she stashed her phone and unrolled more yarn. She accidentally tangled everything together. "Argh! Why does this always happen to me?"

Fiona tsk-tsked. "Remember what I taught you. Yarn only

needs enough slack to work comfortably. Otherwise, it becomes—"

"A knotted mess," Jane finished with a sigh.

"Exactly." Her friend threaded her needles with sure, fluid motions. "Don't let yourself get frustrated. What's our knitter's motto?"

"Whatever it is, it's okay. Knit happens." Jane pulled her needle free of the knot and laughed, because what else could she do?

A whispered curse whipped her attention to Beau. He'd dropped the laptop and scrambled to retrieve it from the floor. His breathing had quickened, and his cheeks appeared flushed.

"Are you all right?" she asked, concerned. She'd requested he stay to speak with Conrad, but what if the poor guy was coming down with a fever? That man cold *was* going around town.

"I'm, uh, fine." He glanced her way, then quickly averted his gaze, returning his attention to the laptop's screen. "The computer is fine, too. Nothing cracked. I'll be more careful."

Yes, but what had caused the drop in the first place?

Fiona patted her hand and whispered, "That boy needs some laughter in his world."

Agreed. But for a start, Jane must get him to crack a smile. She missed the shy but sweet boy he'd been. The friend she'd always craved. What kind of life had he led in their years apart?

The crunch of gravel snagged her attention. A quick glance out the window revealed a dark sedan she would recognize anywhere. Special Agent Conrad Ryan had arrived.

Her pulse raced as he stepped out of the car, tucking his sunglasses into his pocket. No suit today. Instead, he wore a plain T-shirt and jeans. The casual attire looked good on him. Really good. His dark hair appeared windblown, his features stern.

Jane licked her dry lips and rushed to the front door, where she paused to smooth the wrinkles from her dress. Why, why, why did he make her so nervous? Nothing would ever happen between them, probably.

Beau stood and muttered, "If you don't mind, I'm going to use your bathroom." He didn't wait for a response, but marched past her, heading down the hall. Hey, why so jumpy?

Deep breath in. Jane twisted the knob. Hinges creaked, the entrance opening, revealing Conrad as he climbed the steps. Porch light illuminated serious features.

"Welcome back," she said with a little too much force. *Blowing this.* Should she offer to show him the alleged murder weapon or wait for his go-ahead? What kind of hat went with a Tada moment? *Here's your bloodied crowbar.*

He nodded to Jane as he entered the house, the intoxicating scent of cedar and spice making her head fog. But he promptly ignored her. "Good afternoon, Fiona. Nice to see you again."

Um, where was Jane's verbal greeting?

Rolex jumped down and sat at his feet, looking up with falsely adoring eyes. Conrad fell for it, like everyone else, and bent to pet him. Hiss. Swipe. Dart off.

Blood welled on the agent's hand. Two punctures topping two zigging lines. He stared at the injury and smiled. *For-real* smiled. The amusement glittered in his dark eyes. Her heart sped up.

"Nice to see you, too, Rolex," he called, and her chest swelled. But, um, still no greeting for Jane?

Fiona wagged her needles in Conrad's direction. "Are you trying to charm me into whipping up my blueberry pancakes, young man? Aw. You poor thing. Your request is denied for reasons." She humphed and got back to work. "Unless you ask real nice."

"Ask real nice," Jane blurted out. "Please, Conrad." She pressed her hands together, creating a steeple. "There's always time for pancakes."

"I'm sorry, but I'm on the clock."

Noooooo! Why did the universe hate her?

Once again, Fiona looked at Conrad as if he were a disappointment. This time, he noticed.

To lessen the sting of his refusal, he winked at the older woman, and, oh, did he give good wink. "What are you making?"

"They're called funny bunnies." Fiona *humphed* before showing him the perfect white rabbit she'd created in record time. "We donate them to different charities for children. Places that help kids who've lost everything. This might be the only toy the little darlings have for a while."

He jolted, as if the words packed a punch. "You're making a difference in a kid's life. That's…nice."

He sounded genuinely touched. Choked up, even, and affected in a way Jane hadn't expected.

She opened her mouth to ask something. She wasn't sure what. A thousand questions bubbled up. Then he turned those dark eyes on her and her mind blanked. *Think!*

When a guest arrived, a good host offered…*come on, I know this one.* Drinks! Right. "Would you like some sweet tea, Conrad? Agent? Special Agent Conrad."

"No, thank you, Jane. And it's Conrad, remember?"

His voice had dipped, sending shivers down her spine. When his eyelids dipped, too, she gulped. Why this change in his demeanor? What did that hooded look mean? Why were her limbs going weak? Not knowing what else to do, she returned to her rocker.

"And what are *you* making?" he asked her.

"Mine is also a bunny." She tapped her toy with the tip of her needle. "Obviously."

"Ah, yes. *Obviously.* The ears are quite...noticeable. And the colors..."

"I know! I wasn't sure pink, orange and red would go together, but the end result is quite stunning." She examined her adorable creation. It wasn't finished, but it definitely, without question, looked like a bunny. Maybe. Probably. Possibly an elephant with two trunks. "I'll make one for you. To remember me by. Or because it's the polite thing to do. Yes, that one. I'm polite."

He shook his head, the corners of his mouth curving up ever so slightly. "I wouldn't want to deprive a kid of their only toy. Maybe you can teach me to knit so I can contribute to the haul." His biceps flexed as he crossed his arms over his chest. "So, you think you've found the murder weapon?"

Whoa, whoa, whoa. Back up a little. Had he just arranged a future date?

Breathe! "Beau and I discovered a crowbar as we walked the grounds."

His brows drew together. "Is Beau another pet?"

A pet project, maybe. "Beau is not. He's the owner of Peach State Security. A long-lost and recently found friend. We went to school together."

The soldier returned from the bathroom, the three mentions of his name seeming to summon him. He'd splashed water on his face, droplets clinging to his lashes. "That's me. I'm Beau Harden."

Conrad looked between them. "You're staying with Jane?"

"When requested," Beau replied, nodding. "And when needed."

The two males faced off, as if sizing each other up animal-kingdom style.

"That is magnanimous of you," Conrad said.

"Isn't it?" Beau lifted his chin.

Polite words, and yet tension crackled in the air. Rolex sensed it and hissed at a shadow.

Jane glanced at Fiona, hoping for a heads-up about what was transpiring between the two guys, but her friend was too busy trying not to laugh. She probably believed the two men were fighting over Jane. Which kind of made sense. But also mostly didn't make any sense whatsoever. Beau didn't even smile at her anymore, and Conrad sometimes suspected her of murder. Although the special agent did smolder at her upon occasion.

Her pulse leaped. *Focus up!* Time to step in and take over the conversation.

A little nervous but determined, Jane shot to her feet and stepped in the middle of the pair. "Like I was saying, Beau was with me when I spotted the crowbar. I asked him to stick around in case you needed a statement."

Conrad wrote the other guy's address in his notebook and offered a humorless smile. "A statement won't be necessary at this time, Mr. Harden. You are free to leave if you'd like."

Oh no. "I'm sorry I wasted your time, Beau. Please add every second to my bill."

"No problem." Beau gathered his things and left the house. Her determination to find him a girlfriend returned and redoubled. Operation Make Him Smile. He was helping her, so she should help him.

Conrad met and held her gaze, his emotions still erased. "Why don't you take me to the weapon?"

"Yes, of course. I'll just be a moment."

He quirked a brow. "A hat?"

"What can I say? I protect my skin in style." Jane raced up the stairs.

GENA SHOWALTER & JILL MONROE

"Not the purple one. Or the black," Fiona called. "To be safe, pick none of them."

Jane rolled her eyes. Fiona had a serious bias against headwear. Now, then. Which one, which one? The yellow. Definitely. To match her dress. The edges were a bit frayed. So what?

She returned to find an empty living room. Even Rolex had abandoned ship. Her guests, at least, had migrated to the porch. Fiona and Conrad chatted in hushed tones. What in the world could they be discussing?

Though Conrad's expression was harsh, whatever he said charmed the older woman. Fiona smiled and pressed a hand to her heart.

"I'm ready," Jane announced, stepping outside. Warm air enveloped her, the scent of magnolias as inviting as ever.

He glanced in her direction, his eyes glittering with what looked to be mirth. Seriously, what had he and Fiona discussed?

He motioned toward the cobblestone path. "Please. Lead the way."

"Don't forget what I told you, agent," Fiona called as they headed into the thick of the cemetery.

"What did she tell you?" Jane asked as soon as they were out of earshot.

"Several things. The most memorable is the threat to castrate me if ever I'm mean to you."

"Awww." She pressed her hand over her heart, just as Fiona had done. "How sweet is she?"

"The sweetest," he deadpanned, and Jane chuckled. "She also offered me a bit of advice."

"And?" she prompted when he went quiet.

He rolled his eyes. "Vague idea, vague results."

Her brow wrinkled. "What does that mean? Vague idea about what?"

"What I want." Did he give her a pointed glance?

Shivers rained over her. Could Conrad be interested in Jane *romantically*? Despite her name being on the suspect list? Had he been, maybe, *jealous* of Beau earlier?

The moisture in her mouth dried. Nerves suddenly on overdrive, she changed the direction of the conversation. "Will any of the other investigators be joining us?" Should she make a fresh batch of sweet tea?

"Wanted to check things out before bringing a unit out here."

Did he think she'd made a mistake? This might be her first murder investigation, and she might not have any formal or informal training, but...she couldn't remember why this irritated her. Whatever. "What do you know about the fleur-de-lys signs appearing in town?" she asked.

He ignored her question. "Tell me more about the tours you conduct."

Oh. Did he suspect a guest? Or just hope to refocus her attention? "Do you want to know the different kinds I give? What areas of the cemetery I highlight? A list of those who have recently attended?"

"Everything."

He, for sure, suspected a visitor then. Now, she did too. Every. Single. One.

"Well." She cleared her throat to warm up her vocals, getting into guide mode. "In 1829, gold was discovered in the North Georgia mountains. That's when my ancestors moved here from Pennsylvania. Silas Ladling was certain he would find his fortune panning in the babbling brook that runs between Autumn Grove and Eden Valley. Instead, he wound up finding—"

"Jane," Conrad said, the corners of his mouth twitching. "I don't require the cemetery's entire history."

Oh. How disappointing. Giving tours was her sweet spot.

The moment she truly shined. "I'm merely recounting to you what I tell everyone else. If the killer has participated, shouldn't you hear what he or she—or they—heard? I mean, I don't mean to tell you how to run your investigation or anything, but this seems like Solving Crime 101."

Looking as if he stifled a laugh, he nodded. "You're right. Please do continue."

She jumped back in without missing a beat. "Trouble. Silas found a whole lot of trouble. He was ready to pack up his family and move on but suddenly, his fortune turned."

"He struck gold, after all?"

She gave a sad shake of her head. "Unfortunately, no. His luck got even worse. He was shot in a duel. As you can probably guess, duels were outlawed back then. Ladling lore suggests Silas was the first to be buried after Muffin the dog, courtesy of Silas's eldest son. In fact, it's believed the first twenty-three burial plots contain men who died because of gold. I don't know if you've noticed, but Aurelian Hills is mad for the stuff. When Silas's grandson ran the Garden, rumors spread suggesting his father had hidden gold in some of the coffins."

"I can't imagine that was good."

"No," she said with a shrug of her shoulders. "Within a matter of weeks, looters raided every grave. If there *was* gold, it got snatched. Now the Gold Rush Museum is featuring journal passages from different miners who lived back then. I provided a few passages from one of my own ancestors."

If only *she* could find a bit of gold. The Garden of Memories could use an influx of cash right now.

Gold. Hmm. The idea poked and prodded at her. Something there? She stole a glance at Conrad, awed as the sunlight turned his *skin* to molten gold.

"What do you do out here?" he asked. "Exactly."

"For starters, I inherited caretaking duties from my grandma. Lily."

"What happened to your parents?"

"Both are gone," she told him as they rounded a corner.

His rugged features softened. "I'm sorry. I know the pain of losing your family. I was ten when I lost mine."

Sympathy welled, choking her. "Oh, Conrad. That must have been horrible for you." Beyond. He'd said family, not just parents. Who all had he lost? "But, um, I meant neither of them live in Aurelian Hills. Or even Georgia, for that matter. They met and had me while in high school. My dad moved to New Mexico instead of marrying my mom. He's never really been part of my life. My mother wasn't ready for me either, I guess, so Grandma Lily raised me."

Wait. Was she sharing too much? Getting too personal, going too deep? *Stop. Pump the breaks.*

"Pain is pain," he said in a gentle tone.

Well, maybe they could delve a *little* deeper. "Who ended up raising you?"

"The system." Tension radiated from him. "Your mom isn't part of your life now?"

The urge to hug him bombarded her. "She is, and she isn't. When I was three, she relocated to Alabama. She took me with her and tried to be a mother but she struggled. In the end, she shipped me back to Grandma Lily for the summer, and I never left. Now Mom is with a new man and living in Texas with my two half sisters. She calls me sometimes."

Jane offered the information smoothly, pretending not to care. The total rejection from both parents provided more proof of the curse's influence. The two people supposed to love her most had always loved her least. Most days she even convinced herself everything had worked out for the best.

71

But sometimes the pain of it all got the better of her, and she wondered *what if?*

What if her dad had wanted a relationship with her? What if her mom had been less concerned with having fun and more concerned with her little girl's well-being?

"And your dad?" Conrad asked.

"He's not a dad to me but a father." She rubbed a strange tickle at the end of her nose. "He has another family, an ex-wife and three grown sons." Half brothers she'd met only once. She forced a smile. "And that's a wrap on the story of Jane Ladling. We should probably concentrate on the case. That *is* why you're here, and the weapon is around the next corner."

He nodded as if he understood that she'd shared enough for one day and reached her limit. They came upon the flowery arch leading to Muffin's headstone, where Sheriff Moore stood, motioning them over.

Conrad held up a finger, asking for a moment, and stopped with Jane about ten feet away.

Jane had to crane her head to see him past the brim of her hat. A thousand emotions swam in his incredible eyes. Too many to pinpoint a single one.

"Thank you for the escort," he said as those emotions died, one after the other. Soon his expression blanked. "I'll meet you at the cottage when I'm done." He walked away, approaching the sheriff, leaving her behind.

Hello, mixed signals. Sighing, Jane skipped home. Dang. Had the evening grown hotter? When had the moon become such a scorcher?

Fiona hadn't left the porch. The older woman stood at the rail and wagged a finger in her direction as she approached. "You're in trouble, hon."

"Me?" She hiked a thumb at her chest just to be sure.

"You're poking at a bear's cage, and he might be a biter, if you know what I mean."

"No, I do not know what you mean." What bear? What cage?

"I'm not complaining, mind you. It's going to be highly entertaining to watch when he bursts through those bars. And he will. It's only a matter of time now. But you best be careful. I have a feeling you're gonna be the one with the wounds. There will be scars."

Foreboding rocked her. But foreboding was an excellent liar. Fear wrapped in a fancy package. So, she swallowed and marched ahead, doubling down. "What are you even talking about right now?"

"You know exactly what I'm talking about, young lady. Why can't you see that there's no such thing as a curse—"

"Nope. Stop. There *is*."

"—except the ones we place upon ourselves."

"Nope. Wrong again." She would *never* curse herself. Would she? Had she? No! Some people seemed touched by favor, everyone else by favor repellent. And that was a fact.

"Just remember this. Even the smallest bites can fester. Take your Special Agent Ryan for instance. He can charm like no one's business when he puts his mind to it. But there's pain there."

Wait. Was Conrad the bear in this analogy? "No one's biting anyone, Fee." Maybe? Probably? Why did her heart race at the thought?

"Are you sure? Because he's turned down my blueberry pancakes. Twice! That's two strikes against him. One more strike, and I'll erase him from my list of eligible suitors and never set him up with anyone ever again!"

Um... "How many strikes do I have, and what can I do to earn the third?"

"Oh, you hush. You just mind your heart, you hear me, young lady?"

"Yes, ma'am. I'm on guard duty twenty-four seven, trust me. Now start talking and tell me everything you and Conrad discussed in secret." Jane raced up the porch steps, determined to launch a full interrogation. Everything from his tones to his body language and his expressions. Had he executed any side glances? A—

Jane sneezed. Then she sneezed again. And again. The sneezing went on forever and a day.

When, finally, she stopped, her sinuses were swollen shut. Her eyes burned and watered. What in the world?

"Oh no, no, no," Fiona said, backing away from her. "Is the world's most vicious patient getting sick?"

World's most vicious patient? "I'm not that bad," she insisted. But she did want to scream at the top of her lungs.

"I know. You're worse! You morph into a half rage monster, half diaper baby when you're sick."

Rage monster? Diaper baby? As if. First of all, she was as sweet as sugar. Always. Second, she was nothing like those wimps at the clinic. "Good thing I'm not sick then. I'm obviously allergic to something in the air. And I dare *anyone* to say otherwise."

"Sure, sure. I agree with whatever you're saying, hon." Backing away. No, not just backing away but moving toward the door. "I'm gonna gather my belongings now. No sudden movements." Her friend rushed into the house before shooting out, blazing past Jane, calling, "I'm off. I'll see you soon, but probably not too soon. Goodbye for at least a week, hon."

"I'm not sick," she lamented, then sneezed yet again. Surely her trip to the doctor's office—her investigation— hadn't led to illness. But had the temperature just risen a thousand degrees? "I think I'll rest for a couple minutes," she told no one. "But only a couple minutes."

CHAPTER SIX

Daniel Smith
Beloved City Works Employee
One Way. Do Not Enter.
Plot 765, Garden of Memories

*C*olds sucked. Life sucked. Everything sucked, and Jane hated everyone everywhere except Rolex, and only wanted to scream and scream and scream. And also sob. Maybe sleep a while. Or forever.

For an endless eternity—or three days—she existed in a coughing, sneezing void, rising from bed only to feed her precious fur baby. Sometimes strange tones jerked her to attention. Or she rethought her decision to follow Grandma Lily as caretaker and instead focused on a new career in standup comedy, certain she would set the world on fire with her brilliance. She'd already developed a top-ten list on the differences between people who preferred salt and those who favored pepper. A real gut-buster. She just had to remember one or two—or all of them. In her spare time, she imagined talking to Conrad or Beau.

During one of their conversations, Conrad had stayed on the line with her for hours, listening to her complain, because she hadn't wanted to be alone for once. He was so sweet. She missed him *so much*. They should chat again. In her mind, she picked up her cell phone and keyed up his number.

His husky voice purred inside her head. "I hoped you'd call."

Of course he had. Fantasy Conrad couldn't get enough of her. He liked to purr questions into her ear.

Today was no different. "What was your first thought when we met?"

"I think you're so hot," she blurted out. "Hotter than the best chicken noodle soup in the world. Daisy makes it. You should bring me some. It cures everything." She hacked up a lung. "That soup might even solve our case. Tell me everything you know immediately, or we're finished forever!"

"So much to unpack here." How smug he sounded, even in her dream. And why did she ramble in her head? Shouldn't she shine like a bright star *somewhere*?

"If you break my heart, I'm going to break your face." The fervent vow escaped between heaving coughs. Oops. Perhaps Fiona was right; Jane might be evil when sick.

"That is good to know. Listen, sweetheart," Conrad said, his tone softening. "I doubt you'll remember this, but I'm telling you anyway."

Sweetheart? The heat in her veins cooled, shivers cascaded over her limbs. Fantasy Conrad certainly had her number. 1-800-CharmMe.

"We replaced the crowbar on Muffin's marker with a lookalike," he continued. "We also hid some cameras in the area, just in case."

She waited for another endearment. Silence. Disappointment set in. He should call her *sweetheart* all the time. With every sentence he uttered and question he asked. It was practically a declaration of love.

Love.

Jane connected the dots and gasped. "Guess what? You're falling in love with me but should stop 'cause I'm cursed."

"Cursed, huh? I'm intrigued. Tell me more."

She tried to tell him more; she really did. But different words escaped her mouth. "Wouldn't it be amazing if turtles had wings? They would finally have a higher perspective. Wait. Beau traveled the world with the military I bet. What if he saw one?" She hung up on a chuckling Conrad and dialed fantasy Beau.

He answered on the third ring, a hint of amusement in his tone. "Hello, Jane."

"You'd be my favorite smoke show if you'd smile more. Or ever." The words exploded from her, the whatever she'd been thinking about suddenly forgotten. "Don't pick a mean girl as your favorite girl. Am I saying girl too much? Whatever. You gotta pick someone who puts the 'fun' in your funeral. Not that you're dead or anything. But you kind of are."

"That's...good to know?" A pause. Then, "Can you think of *anyone* who matches your description of my perfect girl?"

"Not yet, but I will." She rolled to her side and curled into a ball. "What's your number one requirement for your future girlfriend, anyway?"

A long while passed while Jane relaxed, listening to her breathing.

"Trust. Safety," he groused, jolting her from a daze.

"Yes! You need this. You need this now. Go on a date with the woman of my choice. Please, Beau. Please. I've never asked you for anything. In fact, I'm always telling you *not* to do things."

"Fine, I'll go on a date. But you and the guy of your choice have to double."

Even better. "Deal. Hey, do you ever wonder why June bugs come in May and stay until July?"

Static crackled over the line. "I can honestly say I do not."

Her heavy eyes gained a hundred pounds and drifted shut, different muscles going lax. "Sleepy night-night time now. Zip those adorable lips." Darkness fell over her mind, and she knew nothing more.

On the fourth morning, Jane slowly cracked open her eyes. Oh, wow. Morning sunshine beamed through her bedroom window, but her eyes weren't watering. Acid still leaked into her throat if she dared to swallow, but she wasn't praying for death, so, improvement. Even better, her thoughts were almost clear.

She eased into a sitting position, propped against a mound of pillows. Wadded up tissues and empty juice boxes formed mountains around her. She desperately needed to take a shower.

Memories rose to the surface, and her jaw went slack. No. No, no, no. She hadn't...she wouldn't...she wasn't foolish enough to call the boys and say those kinds of things. She wasn't!

Her stomach churned as she checked her cell phone's call history. Oh, crap. She had. She'd called the boys and asked ridiculous questions. She had admitted *humiliating* things.

Cheeks stinging, she searched the rest of the call log. Fiona had texted every day, worried. And filled with information about Beau and Conrad. Oh, wow. So many words. Jane's eyes glazed over. Something about the boys working together. Maintenance. So kind.

Jane shot her friend a quick text. *It lives! I've risen from the dead and feel almost normal. We can resume business as usual.*

Fiona insta-responded, as if she'd been waiting for this

moment with bated breath. *Oh, praise the Lord! I will alert the troops at once! They've been desperate for the latest word about our patient.*

Her chest suddenly felt a little funny. She might have embarrassed herself, but those guys cared about her. They were her friends. *Good* ones.

And she owed her good friend Beau a date. Excitement bloomed. The guy *needed* an upbeat ray of sunshine. Which meant Jane was already proving herself as a world-class matchmaker. Because yes, she'd pegged him accurately the moment she had discovered him on her porch. Now she only had to whip up a suitable candidate for him and arrange the perfect meet cute, then find *herself* a date.

What was Conrad doing right now? Why not call him and —No! No more phone calls.

Why not make herself useful and learn more about Dr. Hotchkins's volunteer work? Or do some digging about the fleur-de-lys? Either one helped her case. And she needed to help her case. The cold had stolen so much of her time—time the killer had roamed free, unpunished for disrupting life at the cemetery. And for also ending a life.

She took her next dose of cold meds, downed as much water as possible, then propped herself on pillows and settled the laptop on her thighs. She would start with—

Bang, bang, bang. Beau must be hammering something nearby. No doubt Fiona had texted him as promised, informing him of Jane's recovery. Wait. Fiona could have only texted him moments ago. To jump into action so quickly, he must have been at Jane's house already. Waiting on her to heal? But why? He'd already installed the cameras and finished the security work she had yet to pay him for. What else was he doing out there?

Perhaps she would forget her research right now and check the security feed for—

No. No checking on Beau, either. Not now. Investigative work first, extracurricular activities later.

With a little (better-than-expert) sleuthing online, she quickly discovered the name of Dr. Hotchkins's volunteer program. Summerhill Community Pediatric would host a memorial for him this Saturday.

Two days from now. Surely she'd be 100 percent racer ready by then. She could nose around. Maybe she'd find someone at the center who'd also toured the cemetery. Worth a shot, anyway. She hadn't ruled out all the doctor's coworkers.

Bang, bang, bang. Louder than before. Meaning Beau had most likely changed locations. Forget waiting to check on him. What was even going on right now?

She logged into the camera feed on her laptop. As she searched for him, she realized someone had tended to the cemetery while she'd been sick. Nothing was out of place. Not a single weed had been allowed to grow.

Beau and Conrad had done this, hadn't they? Working together, doing maintenance, just as Fiona's texts had claimed.

Maybe they were already fast friends?

Jane discovered the tall Nordic-god-of-old lookalike working on a window shutter for the cottage. Hey! More labor on his part? At a discount, no doubt. Well, no more. No taking advantage of him. So, no home repairs. Except, what if he wasn't doing it for her? Not fully, anyway. What if he attempted to distract himself from his internal struggles? A way to cope?

Her chest clenched. Well, that settled it. There'd be no complaining from her. Let him do what he needed to do. But there'd be no more waiting either. She would find him the perfect woman ASAP.

As she showered, she considered options. By the time she

dried off and dressed in—gasp!—a T-shirt and jeans, she had a pretty good idea where to start. The Headliner.

Feeling better by the hour, Jane searched the local message board, then social media pages. She followed links and connections until she had worked up a list of two eligible bachelorettes for Beau. Eunice Park and Tatiana "Ana" Irons. Jane had attended high school with both girls.

Eunice was the former class vice president, who'd left for Georgia Tech on a soccer scholarship and returned as Aurelian Hill's premier accountant. She even volunteered at the local animal shelter. Who wouldn't love a woman everyone in town trusted with their money? Someone who took care of pre-adopted pets in her spare time?

Ana actually ran the Headliner. The perfect job for her curious nature. In school, she'd taken responsibility for the paper and yearbook, pretending to be a hard-hitting journalist, willing to ask the tough questions. Namely, which students were cheating?

If Jane could convince Beau to go to the community center with her and a double date afterward...if either Eunice or Tatiana happened to be free...talk about the perfect day! But who would be *Jane's* plus one?

Someone appropriate, of course. An acceptable candidate who wasn't investigating her for murder. Ugh. Would she have to ask Fiona for help? Her friend would never let her live it down.

A sharp double knock sounded at the door, and she yelped, startled. A knock she recognized. No. No way. Conrad had not driven out here. Because they lived an hour apart. He had *not* begun the drive before learning she was better. Except, he had.

Her heart tripped as she checked the feed. A familiar SUV was parked in her driveway. Sure enough, Conrad stood at her door. He held a tote bag, and he looked better than ever in a plain white T-shirt and jeans.

Jane leaped from the bed, racing to the vanity. Not that she cared what she looked like, but she freaking cared what she looked like. Okay. All right. Better than expected. Hair mostly air dried. The dark circles under her eyes had faded— slightly. Her formerly bright red nose was now only a vivid pink.

Maybe a hat would complete—no. No hat with jeans. If Conrad truly wasn't a romantic option, his opinion truly didn't matter. She marched to the door, her head high, and opened up.

Perhaps she was a little defensive when she barked, "What?"

He canted his head in that detective-y way of his. If that smile he was fighting won, she might just smack it off.

Oops. She could still be battling her sickbed rage. "I mean, what can I help you with, detective?"

"Oh, wonderful. You didn't threaten to feed me my own organs today." A subtle hint of cedar and spice infused the air between them. "You must feel better. The red nose is a cute touch, though."

How dare he? "It's pink!"

"And the clothes." He slid his gaze over her, and she bowed up, ready to rumble.

"It's my day off."

His gaze moved back up, another fever ravaging her veins. "And that thousand-dollars-an-hour voice."

Her brow furrowed. "That *what?*"

He was absolutely fighting a grin as he swept past her front door, the bag dangling from his fingers.

Wait. Was he bantering with her? Flirting and teasing? "I never said I would feed you your own organs. Did I?"

"You most certainly did," he called from deep inside the house. "Twice."

At least he didn't sound upset about it. If anything, he radiated more amusement.

Living people were so weird. Jane shut the door and tracked him down, Rolex on her heels, furious a man entered his home. They found their guest in the kitchen.

Conrad looked fully at ease as he removed containers from the tote. Jane hadn't seen a man putter around the kitchen since her Pops had died. Jane stopped abruptly, arrested by the sight and scents. The realization. "You went to Daisy's," she gasped out. "Her chicken noodle soup is a magic cure-all for everything wrong in everyone's world."

He plucked a spoon from the bag and placed it on top of a container. "As you told me. A million times."

Oh yeah. She winced. Then she remembered something else and gulped. He'd called her sweetheart. "Just to be clear, you bought chicken noodle soup for me? Jane." *Your sweetheart.* Something only Fiona and Grandma Lily had ever done.

"That *is* what you requested, right?" Conrad tapped the takeout bowl, drawing her attention to the chipped countertop with yellow laminate straight out of 1967.

Stray thoughts bombarded her. What did he think of her home? Where did he live? What decorating styles did he prefer? Had she really asked him to feed her? And he'd *complied?* Was she his "sweetheart" only while sick or also when well? Were they bantering?

Her stomach fluttered. "Thank you, Conrad. I'm speechless."

"Don't say that." He winked at her. Actually winked. "I should be rewarded for my good deed, not punished."

Um. What the *what?*

We are definitely bantering. He *liked her* liked her. Didn't he?

She shook her head like a Magic Eight Ball, an answer rising to the surface. *Seems likely.*

Heart racing, she tripped to the counter and sat in one of the barrel back wooden chairs opposite him, watching him work. The muscles in his forearms rippled, but she *barely* noticed. Honest! "What else did I ask you to do?" What if she'd blocked the truly awful things?

Rolex claimed the chair at her right, eyeing Conrad and brimming with malice. Even if the man *had* brought food.

"Ask? No. You *demanded* I update you on the case. To save my very life, I'm here with information." He pulled a loaf of Daisy's famous sweet bread from the bag and placed it on the cutting board. A family heirloom Jane kept on the countertop, tucked behind the blender. "Here's the thing. I'm human, and I'm due a lunch break. Why not eat it here with you and discuss the investigation? Two birds, one stone. All above board. Mostly. I promise I'll tell you as much as I can."

Soup *and* information? "Yes, please and thank you." She made grabby hands, and he slid her portion closer. A pop of the lid filled the room with a savory blend of herbs and vegetables. Her mouth watered.

"Hungry?" he asked.

"Starved. I didn't know it until this moment." She offered him a smile, determined to keep the emotion out of her eyes. *It's just soup.*

Please. This represented more than just soup—for both of them. But it shouldn't. *Hate the curse!*

Outside, a hammer crashed into a metal toolbox. The clang startled her, and she yelped. A moment later, she spotted Beau through the window. He stalked across the yard, his massive shoulders outlined through thin linen curtains the color of buttercups. Grandma Lily had loved decorating with flower themes to match her name. Jane kept up the tradition, adding violet knickknacks and rose-scented candles.

He slammed the gate of his truck, clearly upset. Why? Was he leaving? But they hadn't discussed the double date yet.

"Butter?" Conrad asked.

She jerked, returning her focus to him. *Eat my meal. Give Beau time to cool down. He'll approach when he's ready.*

"Yes, please," she said. "Like Daisy's soup, butter makes everything better."

"I'm beginning to believe there are people who make everything better too." His gaze lowered to her lips. "What do you think?"

Had he referenced her? "Um. Maybe?"

Conrad seemed to give himself a shake before pushing his soup to the other stool. He stalked around the counter and sat beside her. "The case. We're pursuing a couple different leads and motives and questioning several people of interest."

"Oh?" She propped her elbows on the countertop and dropped her chin on the back of her hands. "Tell me more," she said, mimicking him.

He took his sweet time, using a plastic knife to slather the bread with the creamy butter provided in a small cup. "The doctor had an active sex life outside of his marriage. Many of those women had a boyfriend or husband. On the other hand, we found evidence to indicate the doctor had recently developed a passion for hunting treasure."

"So the motive is love or money." Just as her research predicted. She was *nailing* this investigation.

"The motive is *always* love or money. One or the other."

"I don't understand what either has to do with the cemetery, though. I mean, a graveyard rarely evokes feelings of romance or greed."

"You'd be surprised," he muttered.

Had he investigated other cemetery murders? Or was he referring to the here and now?

The edge in his voice kind of sounded more *personal*, and she grew flustered.

"And treasure?" she continued, sinking her spoon into the hearty soup. Steam coated the air, creating a dreamy haze. "Everyone knows the cemetery was once raided and stripped of any hidden gold. Unless new rumors surfaced?" What if someone had remembered the gold but forgotten the raid?

He remained silent for a moment. Gave a little huff. "Has anyone mentioned anything about a connection between the fleur-de-lys that's been showing up around town and the legends about the gold?"

Her eyes widened. "No." But was there? There must be. She would swear—yes! Dots began to connect. The fleur-de-lys, connected to the legends of gold. She *had* seen the symbol before, or something like it, somewhere. But where? The gold exhibit? Her family's records? Both? Neither?

Conrad leaned over and gently nudged her shoulder with his own. "C'mon. Finish your soup, and I'll show you what I ordered for dessert."

Dessert! Gimme! Jane blew on a spoonful of broth before tasting. An explosion of flavor drew a moan from her. She closed her eyes and savored. Warmth spread through her.

A thought caught her off guard, and she couldn't not ask. "Why are you being so nice to me, Special Agent Conrad Ryan?"

He lifted a brow. "Am I usually cruel to you?"

"You're usually closed off. Which is cruel to someone like me. So yes. You are usually cruel to me." But there had been those few glimpses at an ooey-gooey center beneath his hard candy shell.

"Let's say my job leaves me unnaturally suspicious of

everyone I meet. The actions they make. The words they use. Having a traumatic childhood doesn't help matters."

An ache stung the back of her throat, and it had nothing to do with her waning cold. What terrible things had young Conrad survived?

That he was opening up to her, sharing even the smallest bits and pieces about his life, affected her. Something told her he didn't do this often. But what had brought on this change? And how should she respond? Would he shut her out if she pressed for more?

"Conrad—"

"Nope. I'm done." Motions as brisk as his tone, he closed what remained of his soup.

Fine. Maybe he'd finished talking, but Jane had only begun to offer comfort. She reached out slowly. He let her. *Contact*. Her breath hitched. They were skin to skin. Heat to heat.

She trailed her fingers from his knuckles to his forearm, lightly stroking him. The muscles tensed beneath her touch. Conrad readjusted, moving out of reach, and her hand plopped to the counter. Where it belonged. She'd overstepped, hadn't she?

"Ready for dessert?" he asked as her cheeks heated. Once again, he donned an emotionless mask. And yet, he flexed his hand before leaning over to free a batch of old-fashioned peanut butter cookies from the tote.

Trying to stop himself from touching her? Wait, who cared about illicit caresses right now? Cookies! "It's as if you can read my mind," she said, snatching a cookie from his grip.

The corner of his lip quirked. "I think I can do anything *but* that. Reading you is tough. You show too much and too little at the same time. I've never struggled to read *anyone* like this."

He must be teasing, and she laughed. Her? Difficult? She was an open book.

A knock sounded on her back door, and she jolted. Dang, she startled easily lately.

"Beau?" Conrad asked with an arched brow.

"Hopefully." Cookie in hand, she hopped off her chair and opened the door. Sure enough, Beau stood there, shifting from leg to leg, discomfort stamped on his features. He held a small container.

"Hi," she said, happy to see him. "Please, come in."

"No, thank you." He looked at Conrad, who leaned against the kitchen wall, watching, and he nodded a greeting. "I saw his car and thought you might need support."

Well. There he was again. The sweet boy determined to protect his childhood friend. She smiled in thanks. "That's so kind, but I'm great. Conrad brought my favorite soup. We've been discussing the case."

"How are you feeling? Truly?" Beau asked.

"Good enough to remember our deal. Don't think you're getting out of it. Oh! While I've got you, we need to discuss the bill you haven't given me."

He rocked on his heels before stepping back. "Just haven't gotten around to it yet."

Or he had no plans of charging her? "Beau, I insist on paying. And don't forget to put your sign at the gate. If you haven't already." She hadn't checked the grounds for days. No telling what changes awaited her out there. "Are you sure you don't want to come in? We can discuss the coming date—"

"This is for you," he interjected. He thrust the round container her way. "I brought you soup as well."

Super sweet? No. The super sweetest! "Thank you, Beau. I love it."

He blinked at her. "You haven't even tasted it. It's not from Daisy's. I, uh, made it. On my own."

From scratch soup? Super sweeter than the super sweetest! "It smells delicious, and now I have dinner. So about that deal. You're keeping your end of the bargain, yes?"

"I'll call you about the date, okay?" he said, spinning and hurrying away. He disappeared around the house. Heading for the front, where his truck was parked?

"I consider that a definite yes," she called after him. Before he could reply with a refusal, she shut the door.

"Date?" Conrad asked, walking over.

She turned and faced him, then leaned against the wall, keeping a few feet of distance between them. "A double. Hey, speaking of, do you know a single man who might be willing to have dinner with me? Unless this is a conflict of interest?"

"I'm still confused." He crossed his arms over his chest. "Double date?"

"I'm setting Beau up with this really great girl, possibly, but he insists I bring a date too. Therefore, I'm on the prowl."

"He insists," Conrad echoed.

"I think he's shy, and I'm a safety net." Maybe. "Everyone needs a support system." And moments ago, Beau had been willing to be hers. Right now, she held his homemade soup in her hands. So yes, she would be his support—his friend— in return.

"I get that. But why do you want to meet one of my friends?" Hard tone. Harder glint in his eyes.

Was he jealous again possibly?

Her heart thudded, and she shuffled around him to set the new soup on the counter. But she didn't take her seat. She kept her back to him. This was about to turn embarrassing, but she decided to spill the truth. "No one in town is interested in me and that's okay, because I'm not interested in any of them either. Truth be told, I'm pretty anti-relationships."

"Explain," he said before she could continue.

Well. He asked for it so... "I'm a victim of the Ladling curse, and that's all I'm willing to say."

He moved directly behind her, the scent of spice enveloping her, leaving her weak in the knees. She breathed deep.

Conrad sifted a lock of her hair between his fingers. "One day soon, we'll dissect this curse together. I want every detail, and you'll give them to me. But I won't be introducing you to any of my friends, Jane. When you go on that double date with Beau, I will be at your side. Me."

Her mouth parted and for a heart-stopping moment, Jane thought Conrad might spin her around and kiss her.

In the end, he put his lips at her ear and rasped, "Goodnight, sweetheart." Then he stalked out of her house, leaving her reeling.

CHAPTER SEVEN

Anne Mathis
Shhh, I'm sleeping.
Plot 859, Garden of Memories

*F*rom bad to better to the best.

Jane occupied the passenger seat of Beau's pickup truck. Muted sunlight filled the cab, filtered through the thousand layers of dust that covered every window. On both her left and right, trees whizzed past. Cars, too. Behind the steering wheel, Beau brooded at a level of ten on a scale of five. The perfect amount. Not too much, not too little.

He'd kept his word and called this morning. Plus, he'd agreed to her plan. Everything from the trip to SCP—Summerhill Community Pediatric—to the date with Eunice Park or Ana Irons. He hadn't even protested more than a dozen times.

Protests her deepest fears echoed. No, no. Not fears. Wisdoms. Experience told her: *Don't take Conrad.*

But a new voice rose from the shadows. Hope whispered, *Give him a shot.*

If she guarded her heart, keeping it locked inside a concrete cage, she probably wouldn't encounter any problems. Except, what if there was already a crack spreading through the cement?

Goodnight, sweetheart.

"Explain why we're doing this again." Beau merged the truck onto the highway, picking up speed.

Jane pulled her thoughts from the seductive purr of memory and focused on the matter at hand. "The murder victim volunteered at SCP. I'd like to question other volunteers and patients about their thoughts of him. Who slept with him or heard rumors about someone else who did, and whether or not they ever hunted treasures with him. But that's all."

"Oh, *that's* all?"

His dry tone drew a laugh from her. "We're also having fun," she said. "Well, as much fun as we can at a memorial service. And I can't thank you enough for doing this. For everything." When she'd gotten sick in the past, she'd phoned a temp agency or put a Closed sign on the door, and let the place handle itself.

"I had the time. No big deal."

Wrong. Big deal. Huge. "You deserved to be paid for your work, Beau. Please, I'm begging you, give me a bill." Did he think he owed her for something in their childhood?

"Sure," he said, but she didn't believe him.

Frustrating man! "In the meantime," she said with a firm nod, "I'm buying your lunch and filling your truck with gas, and I won't hear any arguments on the matter. I'm also planning the best double date in the history of histories. In fact, I've already found your perfect match." Why not rip the bandage?

His brows dropped. "My match?"

"She's amazing, I swear! You will love her, probably.

She—"

"No, don't tell me." He gave a clipped shake of his head. Already nervous? "I'll learn what I need to know on the date. Are you bringing Conrad?"

She bit her lip and ran a finger along her seatbelt. "Yes. I think so. Yes."

A stilted pause before he grudgingly admitted, "I don't hate him. He's not a terrible guy."

They really had worked together. "What changed?"

"I had a friend look into him. He's well-respected. Known for being honest, even when it hurts. A loner "

"Wait. Why did you have your friend look into him?"

"What about the Ladling curse?" he said in lieu of an answer.

Had she spilled her greatest flaw to him, too? "First of all, I said I wanted to *date* Conrad, not marry him, so the curse has no bearing on the situation," she sputtered. "I'm never getting married. I'll bask in the love glow of other couples. What about you? Willing to take the plunge one day?"

He drew in a breath. "Let me think about my answer before I respond."

"Think away. I have my own thoughts to unravel." Except, for once she didn't.

Jane peered out the window the rest of the drive, watching trees and cars whiz past, enjoying the reflective silence. As Beau parked across from their destination, she studied the center. Not what she expected. A large metal building, almost a barn, complete with shuttered windows and a wraparound porch. Lush green grass. A smattering of rose bushes and peach trees. Looked like a home away from home, a farmhouse with an edge. A handful of cars peppered the parking lot, a cluster of women dressed in black making their way inside.

She had opted to wear black as well. A more form-fitting

dress than usual, sewn by Grandma Lily. Her *I am an independent woman, take me seriously* outfit. Best to blend in with confidence when you were crashing a memorial.

"Stay there. Don't move." Beau exited and rounded the car. The sunlight loved him more than ever, the gold in his skin and hair almost otherworldly. He wore a white button-down and dark slacks, his soldier's body stretching the material.

Jane bet Eunice or Ana ended up feeling incredibly safe with him. As the couple built something lasting, Jane wouldn't have to worry about losing everything just as things got good; unlike Jane, Eunice and Ana had a bright romantic future ahead.

Why, why, why must curses be real?

As Beau opened her door and offered her a hand, his expression remained as warm as the spring day. Fiona would be cheering his impeccable manners.

"Thank you," she said, cupping her fingers to his and beaming as he helped her exit. "Come on." She hooked her arm through his and urged him forward. "I'm counting on you to charm and distract every woman we encounter so I can unearth their deepest, darkest secrets."

"Then you brought the wrong guy. Charm isn't my strong suit."

"No offense, but that might be the most ridiculous thing you've ever said. Charm comes in many forms, my friend, and with you, grumpy is one of them. You are absolutely adorable when you brood. Yes, just like that. See?" She patted his cheek. "Adorable."

He blinked down at her with a comical mix of incredulity and—dare she believe it?—amusement. "Adorable. Me. That's a first."

They entered the reception area. As if drawn by an invisible force, she zoomed her attention to the back of the room, where a buffet table of snacks waited. Mmm. Finger sandwiches, the best of all sandwiches. Cookies. Cupcakes. Chips and dip. Her empty stomach grumbled, and she licked her lips.

Inner shake. People first, food second. Right. Bouquets of flowers abounded, perfuming every inhalation. Long tables displayed pictures of Dr. Hotchkins, both from his personal life and his job. Oh! How perfect.

Roughly thirty mourners milled around. Some grouped together, chatting about the doctor. Others remained alone, smiling or crying while studying the photos. Jane found every single one of them suspicious in some way or another. Especially those two. The most intent studiers. She'd memorized the face and bio of every employee listed on the clinic's website. Now, she had only to insert herself—oh crap!

"Conrad," she whispered. Her pulse leaped, and her stomach fluttered. He was here, looking drool-worthy in a suit and tie, and he stared right at her. He'd told her not to investigate, yet here she was, investigating.

Her mouth opened while his lips pressed together in a thin line.

He dragged a heating gaze down her dress. When he met her eyes once again, his irises were ablaze and hot enough to torch her composure. She halfway expected him to stomp across the room and throw her over his impressively wide shoulder. Which she absolutely positively would not enjoy, probably. Instead, he raised his chin and returned his attention to his companion. Another employee she recognized. Dr. Diana Williams. An attractive, forty-something general practitioner who specialized in chronic conditions. One of Dr. Hotchkins's side slices?

"Your agent noticed you the moment you walked in," Beau told her.

He did? If she hadn't waxed poetic about the sandwiches,

she might have noticed him right away too. "Help me avoid him, okay? He'll tell me to leave the moment he's near me."

"That," Beau replied, suddenly vibrating with amusement, "I can do."

He wasn't wrong. He dodged and evaded, and he did it well. As Jane made several passes around the room, speaking to different people, sneaking notes into her investigation pad, Beau ran interference.

Something she learned for their efforts: She had no stealth. Dr. Hotchkins had been adored or hated and nothing in between. Everyone he'd ever encountered had a motive— more than she'd realized in the beginning. Jane was now addicted to cucumber sandwiches, and the doctor had always brought a nurse to SCP. Usually the same one. A woman matching Emma Miller's description, who just happened to go by the name of Nurse Emma. Once, the two were caught kissing after hours.

Affair confirmed and then some.

"—wanted to know about a time this drunk lawyer stormed into the clinic and punched the doctor in the face," the person beside Jane was saying. Oh right. She was in the middle of eavesdropping on a gossip session between a volunteer who had worked alongside Dr. Hotchkins.

Who had wanted to know about the lawyer? Conrad?

"How terrible," the girlfriend said. "Did anyone ever identify the assailant?"

"No. Dr. Hotchkins refused to press charges."

A lawyer? Emma's husband, perhaps? Anthony Miller. The couple had just solidified their place as number one and two on her lists of suspects. Circled, underlined and surrounded by stars.

Emma and Dr. Hotchkins. A woman capable of betraying her husband might not shy away from murder if, say, her doctor lover refused to leave his wife for her.

As Jane's stomach rumbled, she cast a glance to Beau. He stepped in front of Conrad and crossed his arms. The perfect distraction. She worked her way to the snack table for a quick recharge. A moment to get her thoughts together.

Already she could visualize what had happened the night of the murder. After Dr. Hotchkins and Emma got caught at the clinic—the reason for the uproar among staff—they needed a new location to conduct their affair. Somewhere their spouses wouldn't think to look. What better spot than a cemetery? Except the husband had been suspicious of his wife's extracurricular activities for weeks. He followed her and seized the first opportunity to strike, surprising the couple as they desecrated a grave. Hubby Dearest knocked out his wife, killed the doctor and dug up the burial plot, planning to hide the body inside the casket. But something interrupted him.

Or maybe Emma had learned of the doctor's other women and snapped. Maybe she'd planned the whole thing, with or without her husband's aid.

Then, she or they started spray painting the fleur-de-lys on everything, hoping to throw people off their trail. A good plan. Get everyone's mind on gold instead of romance. Or possibly things were reversed, and the romance had been meant to distract from the gold. So many possibilities, all of them one hundred percent valid and without (many) flaws.

Think. What did Jane know about Mr. Anthony Miller? For starters, his face occupied several benches in town. Fiona often touted him as an ambulance chaser. Interviewing him might be tough. A death had occurred, and he had a connection to the victim. As an attorney, he knew better than anyone that his name automatically rose to the top of the suspect list. But for the sake of Jane's reputation, she had to try.

Beau rushed up behind her, startling her. "Incoming," he said. "I couldn't hold him off any longer."

Jane straightened and twisted with a snap, bringing the last four cucumber finger sandwiches with her. "But I'm not...my food—" A scowling Conrad approached.

She shoveled two of the treats into her mouth, barely chewed, and swallowed, destroying the evidence of her greed. As a mix of foreboding, excitement and heat zipped over her nerve endings, she pasted on a bright smile.

His burning gaze remained fixed on her. "What are you doing here, Jane?"

"Don't answer that," Beau advised, maintaining his post behind her.

She frowned at them both before concentrating on the agent. As she and Conrad sized up each other up close and personal, she finished off another sandwich and stayed as cool as, well, a cucumber.

He waited her out, saying nothing.

"Am I committing a crime, officer?" she finally asked.

"It's detective—" He blinked. "It's special agent. And you tell me. *Are* you committing a crime?"

"No?" Was she? Who knew anymore? "I'm performing a public service. In fact, I already have a lead in our case."

"My case. Mine." He stepped closer, a slow ease into her space. "You will not follow this lead, Jane. Say it. Let me hear you."

"But you haven't even heard my idea yet," she said, his scent hitting her. Oh, sweet goodness. So freaking good. Her eyelids dipped as heat washed over her.

"I don't need an explanation. I can guess. You suspect Emma Miller's husband, and you're planning to speak to him. But you won't do it, because I'm telling you not to. You will not visit his office, and you most definitely will not show up on his doorstep. I mean it, Jane."

"Not bad, Officer Detective Special Agent Conrad Ryan." She added just enough sneer in her voice to let him know he could take his silent intimidation and shove it. And yeah, sure, also her deepest defenses had been pricked. He'd used her name twice in two minutes, a bad sign. Clearly he was beyond irritated with her. The first clue that their breakup loomed. Before their first date!

If ever she fell in love with him? Which she wouldn't do. Nope. Not her.

"Jane," he grated.

"All right. Fine. You win, okay? I won't drop by Mr. Miller's office or show up on his doorstep." Truth.

Instead, she would approach him somewhere else. Did Mr. Miller workout at the town's only gym? Frequent a favorite restaurant? Attend the theater? People bumped into each other all the time. Hardly a big deal.

"Now, if you'll excuse us..." She backed up a step, bumping into Beau, who rested a hand on her lower back to stop her from falling.

"Jane." Conrad's annoyance had only sharpened.

"Nope, no need to continue saying what you're saying. Trust me. I've already deduced the highlights. You meant every word. I'll be in huge trouble if I disobey. And finally, I better go home and stay there or else." She spread her arms wide and rolled her eyes. "See? I can detective like a boss, too."

"And if the killer decides to go after *you*?"

Was this an attempt to scare her? "There's no stronger motivation to catch the fiend as quickly as possible."

He pursed his lips and switched his gaze to Beau. "You'll keep her safe?"

Gold-star solve for Conrad. He suspected her of misleading him, and he was taking measures to ensure her well-being, anyway. Her chest clenched with the realization, but that was okay. Because it meant nothing. Less than nothing, most likely.

"I will," Beau vowed. "I'll take a bullet for her if necessary."

What? "No one is taking a bullet for anyone." But awww. How sweet. He cared about her well-being, just as she cared about his. Because they were the best of friends.

Look at that. She now had a buddy at her side and a short-term boyfriend on the horizon. Maybe. Possibly. Either way, things were looking up for this Ladling girl.

A silent exchange seemed to transpire between the guys. That, she didn't like. What were they saying without saying it?

As Beau led Jane to the door, she cast a glance over her shoulder. Conrad stared at her, hard, never pulling his gaze, even when people passed between them. As if she held him captive, and he couldn't muster the strength to look anywhere else. What a powerful thought.

She smiled as she settled into the truck.

"What now?" Beau asked.

Good question. She fished her phone from her purse and hunted for Anthony Miller's information on the internet. According to his social media, he'd just checked into a hotel bar only twenty minutes from their current location to celebrate his upcoming divorce.

"That look on your face leads to trouble," Beau said, sounding resigned. "But go ahead. Tell me. What are we doing next?"

"Interrogating a lawyer over cocktails."

THERE HE WAS. Anthony Miller. He hunched over the hotel bar, alone, swirling amber liquid in a short, round glass. Shadows and light twined over him. Mostly shadows. Dark gray walls and low-burn candles provided a dimming effect. Soft music played in the background. Only a few other people occupied the space.

He looked anywhere from forty to sixty. His mostly pepper hair was disheveled, some of the short strands like spikes. Strain etched lines around his eyes and mouth. A wrinkled shirt was half tucked and half untucked. He had only rolled up one sleeve.

Jane closed the distance before Beau attempted to talk her out of this. He remained close to her heels. At the bar, he darted ahead to pull out a chair for her—a chair two barstools over from Miller. Dang him. She'd hoped to snag the spot at the lawyer's side. Nothing she could do now but accept.

Beau, the most terrible partner in non-crime ever, claimed the seat between them, putting himself closer to the man Jane *would* be questioning.

She leaned into her companion, breathing in a scent so different from Conrad's but just as amazing, and whispered, "You are the best and worst friend of all time. You know that, right?"

He bent his head to hers and whispered back, "You are the oldest friend I have, and I will always put your safety first."

Gah! How could she remain annoyed with him now?

Mr. Miller sneered at them. "You guys in love?" He slurred his words.

Already drunk? Perfect. Jane all but leaped over Beau to get closer to Mr. Miller. "Define love."

"The biggest mistake anyone anywhere can make," he grumbled, then tossed the rest of his drink down the hatch. He focused on her while swaying in his seat, frowned and pointed. "You're familiar to me. Why are you familiar?"

Rather than admitting they lived in the same small town, she said, "Hi, I'm Jane."

"Tony," he muttered.

Beau urged her into her chair and ordered sweet teas for the two of them—teas she would be paying for.

"I gotta say, Tony, your definition of love is, um, unique," she said. "Are you having relationship troubles?"

Beau arched a brow at her, all *you did* not *just blurt that out.* What? She'd cut straight to the heart of the matter.

"Oh, I'm having troubles all right." Tony ordered himself another round. The dirtiest martinis they had. "My soon-to-be ex-wife cheated on me with her boss. Someone killed the guy. I hope they made it hurt." His beverage arrived, and he downed it, too.

Okay. Wow. He'd answered so swiftly and eagerly, as if the words had been poised at the end of his tongue for ages and he'd only awaited a listening ear. Or he'd realized who she was and brilliantly laid a foundation to fit his innocence.

"You know what we should do for revenge?" she said. "Spray-paint something on your wife's car." She winced inside at her poor and abrupt delivery. Oh, well. Onward and upward. "Do you happen to have any cans of spray paint handy? We can help you."

"Nope." He belched into his fist and laughed. "Do you smell that?"

No, he wasn't laying a foundation for anything. Was he guilty of being disgusting? Yes. But he might not be guilty of murder. Emma maintained the number one spot.

Maybe the doctor had ended things with her, and the rejection fueled a rage. Or maybe the reason was something else entirely. Maybe Emma wasn't even involved. But either way, Jane wished to talk to the nurse again.

Looked like she'd be paying the clinic another visit.

CHAPTER EIGHT

William King
What matters? My foes died first.
Plot 211, Garden of Memories

The next day, Jane followed an older, no-nonsense woman through GBH headquarters in Atlanta. People milled around a maze of desks, some in uniform, some not. The scent of coffee infused every breath. Phones rang constantly. A big white board with bullet point descriptions and photos dominated half a wall, just like she'd seen on TV.

She bit back her excitement as her guide stopped in front of a closed door.

"Here you are. The office of Special Agent Conrad Ryan. Good luck," the woman added in a murmur before striding off.

Was the agent in a foul mood because of Jane's conversation with Mr. Miller?

Nerves twisted her stomach. She knew beyond any doubt

the coming meeting would either rock her nonexistent socks off or knock her for a loop.

He'd called her bright and early this morning to ask if raising his blood pressure was a new game she played. She didn't want to believe Beau had snitched on her but...she kind of believed Beau had snitched on her. The two were clearly allies now.

When she'd asked straight up, Conrad had redirected the conversation, telling her nothing. While she'd had him on the line, however, she'd invited herself to his office for a tour. Even though it was Sunday, the Lord's day, he'd agreed.

"Are you planning to stand outside or come in?" Conrad called from inside the office.

"I'm debating." Had she made a mistake coming here? She might have scored a tour *and* a scolding.

Finally, she turned the knob. Her hand trembled. Head high, she swept into the room. The door closed behind her, sealing her within the agent's private domain. He sat behind a nondescript, government-issued wooden desk, but she didn't face him. Not yet. She examined the bigger-than-expected space instead. A large window overlooked the parking lot, where a Georgia state flag rippled in a mild wind. Only a few framed certifications decorated the walls. Or photos. None on the desk. Or anywhere. Huh. Not of his family and friends. Not of anyone.

What did this mean? She'd seen personal photos on the desks she'd passed, which meant displaying of mementos wasn't against governmental policy. The lack was by Conrad's choice. But why?

He'd mentioned a rough childhood. Was he alone now? She didn't mean to, but she flattened a hand over her chest. Was Conrad lonely? Her gaze zoomed back to him, and she gulped. He watched her with more intensity than ever.

Her heart leaped. He wore a dark suit and a fierce scowl.

The imposing man rose to his feet and looked her over. Perspiration glazed her palms. For today's mandatory meeting, she'd chosen a short black-and-white dress. Her favorite. Maybe she'd taken a little extra time with her hair. And actually applied makeup. Mascara. Blush. Lip gloss. What did he think?

"Sit." He motioned to the two chairs in front of his desk. Sharp tone, choppy action. Someone was not happy.

Wait. Sit? "What about the tour?"

He arched a brow, a man assured of his power. "There won't be a tour."

What? "But I want to see the crime lab."

"Then you should have gone home after the memorial service. GBH tours are only offered to well-behaved murder suspects." His dry tone took the sting out of the label.

"Guess that means the cybersecurity unit is out, too," she grumbled, trudging over to slump into the chair. Jane didn't expect a response, and he didn't give her one. "Am I here so you can scare me straight?"

"Someone needs to."

Well, it wouldn't work. She would be visiting Caroline Whittington and Emma Miller for a follow-up appointment, as planned, and that was that. Instincts she hadn't known she possessed were screaming, *So close to the truth!*

His scowl deepened. "You have no business following leads. You'll only go down the wrong roads, because you aren't privy to all the facts."

"You're right. I'm not privy to all the facts. And I think we can both agree that's one hundred percent your fault. But I'm from the town, and I know the people. I'm a resource. Why aren't you making use of me? Think about it. You're a straight line, and I'm a squiggly one. More creative. I can help you see things from a different perspective."

"Like the flying turtles." He steepled his fingers and

105

sighed. "Go on. Elaborate."

Now we're cooking with gas. She scooted to the edge of her seat. "Well, I've already worked up multiple motives for multiple people. I'm sorry to say I've just thought of one for you. And it checks out. Solidly. The logic is bulletproof."

He reclined in his chair, appearing more at ease. Even amused? "Please. Do tell."

Warming up to the topic, she leaned toward his desk. "Picture this. Weeks before the murder, you passed through my town, spotted me, and instantly became obsessed with me." Stranger things had happened. "You would have settled for any excuse to spend time with me. When you couldn't think of one, you supplied one with murder." Her *gotcha* tone drew a grin from him. A there-and-gone grin, but a grin all the same.

He rubbed his fingers over his mouth, eyes crackling with mirth. "Your bulletproof logic has a hole. The day we met is the first I'd heard of your town."

"So you say. We both know murderers can be liars, too. But okay. Let's pretend you're telling the truth. That just means you saw my picture online and hired an assassin to provide the excuse. Though I notice you aren't disputing your attraction to me," she pointed out.

"I don't think anyone can dispute my attraction to you, Jane." He offered the mind-blowing statement casually before he continued on as if nothing had happened. "I gained permission to share other case details with you. But." He pegged her with a hard stare. "I won't be doing so until you agree to stop speaking with people of interest." He extended his arm to offer her a stack of photos. "Consider the acceptance of these images agreement."

Fighting to maintain her composure—*just breathe!*—she did, in fact, accept the stack. But accept his terms? No. Every image showcased a paper on display at the museum's permanent mining exhibit, *Gold Fever!* Exclamation point included. The exhibit kicked off two years ago and quickly became a town staple.

"Wait." Back to gold rather than romance? "The fleur-de-lys. Do you think those are merely a decoy meant to distract from the murder? That Dr. Hotchkins was hunting for gold at my cemetery?"

"It's a possibility." Conrad stood, strode around the desk and sank into the chair at her side. A stronger hit of his dry cedar and spicy scent infused her next inhalation, and she nearly whimpered. So good!

Leaning over, his shoulder brushing against hers, he pointed to a highlighted name—Rhonda Burgundy. Plot 39. The spot Dr. Hots died. "Burgundy's coffin was raided in the past, suspected of holding bricks of gold. She's mentioned at the exhibit. So are several of your other residents. Maybe the doctor believed a stash of gold was overlooked during the raid."

"That rumor has surfaced in the past, but longtime residents know it's false. Dr. Hotchkins is a longtime resident."

Conrad hiked a shoulder. "We believe he planned to meet a woman the night of his murder, but we don't know which, only that she was a regular tap—his words, not mine. He tracked those regulars with a coded calendar in his office. We've identified some but not all."

Women reduced to a code? Gross. "How many, um, taps, are there?"

"Eight. With an assortment of semiregulars and one-night stands mixed in. From what we've pieced together, he used the exam rooms as five-minute motels."

Jane cringed, remembering every instance she'd lain upon a petri dish—er, exam table. "Was Emma Miller one of the known regulars? Because they were definitely having an affair."

"Yes. But her alibi checked out." With a harder tone, he added, "And so did her husband's."

Her first genuine theory went up in smoke. Time to go back to the drawing board. "Give me a chance to identify the unknowns in Dr. Hotchkins's code. If his identifiers reflect traits about the women, I'll recognize—"

"No. I'm sorry, but that's out of the question." Even harder tone.

She didn't have to wonder why. "You think I might be a member of his rotation? I assure you, I'm not. The doctor wasn't my type. Which is unwaveringly single."

Conrad appeared chagrined, even irritated. "Until we've successfully identified everyone, I'm not allowed to fully rule anyone out."

"Why are you sharing *any* case details with me, then, if I'm still a suspect?" Unlike Nurse Emma, Jane couldn't alibi out unless someone learned to speak Meow and Rolex corroborated her story.

Conrad's phone rang, but he ignored it. His expression softened. "I know what it's like to feel as if questions claw at your mind, and I swear to you I will figure this out. You'll have your answers. Just give me time. And peace. I'll work faster—better—if I'm not always worried about you."

She had to hand it to him. It was a nice speech and almost convinced her to back off the investigation. But she wasn't the one responsible for his worry. That was all Conrad.

"I have a better idea," she said as she stood. "You learn how to do deep-breathing exercises to control your fear for my well-being, and I'll continue to aid you." As he glared at her, she smiled sweetly. "Thanks for the nontour, Special Agent Ryan. Let's not do it again soon."

J<small>ANE PONDERED</small> all things Conrad the entire hour-long drive home. She only paused after gassing up and phoning Fiona to let her friend know she was running a few minutes late for their knitting hour.

The agent had admitted to his attraction to her, and he'd made tentative plans to join her on a double date. His boss might suspect her of murder, but Conrad didn't. He liked her as much as she liked him. But she had to wonder: Did he hope to fall in love one day and get married?

Would she lose another guy to the Ladling curse? Guilt flared. Should she even risk dating him? The guy had lost his family as a kid. She might cause more trouble than she was worth.

By the time she parked in her driveway, she was a legit ball of stress. To give him a shot, to not give him a shot? To run away from him or to him? She would have to decide soon. Or the decision would be made for her.

She frowned when she noticed Fiona rushing from one side of the porch to the other, frantically waving her arms.

Stomach dropping, Jane bolted out of the car and hurried over. "What's wrong?"

Features glazed with panic, the older woman grabbed her shoulders and shook. "I planned to wait for you on the porch, but your front door was ajar. I called for Rolex, but he didn't come. I searched but...he...he's probably just exploring."

Her door had been open? Jane remembered closing and locking it as always. Right? She *had* been preoccupied with Conrad. "Y-yes, you go search the grounds. I'll look in his favorite hiding spots."

"Don't worry, hon. Everything will be all right. We'll find him." Fiona rushed off as swiftly as her old bones allowed.

Jane sprinted into the house. Barreled through every room. Checked under every raised surface. Scanned inside every nook and cranny. No sign of her house panther anywhere. When had he left and what direction had he gone?

Think. The camera feed! Jane returned to her bedroom and fired up her laptop, loading today's recording. Slowly fast-forwarding...*There!* A hand flew up to cover her gaping mouth, her heart slamming into her ribs. A woman approached the front door. She wore a dark jacket with a hood, and she maintained a swift pace. From this angle, Jane couldn't see her face.

She noted what details she could. Slender. Average height. A skeleton mask often seen at Halloween hid her features. Locks of brown hair struck out through the sides of the hood. Real or from a wig? The hood remained in place throughout her crime spree, so it was impossible to tell. Considering she'd covered all her bases, the offering of a false clue seemed well within her wheelhouse.

In other words, the hair told Jane nothing about her intruder. An intruder who might have stolen her cat. Acid burned her chest, her throat. If this person had harmed Rolex...

The woman opened the locked door with ease—because she had a key. Jane panted as she disappeared inside the house. Time stamp: two hours and thirteen minutes ago.

Sixty seconds passed, and nothing happened.

Another thirty.

The woman flew out the front door, her hood still in place. Rolex shot from the entrance, hot on her heels. Jane jolted. He lived! And he must be on the grounds as Fiona suggested. Protecting his home.

Jane grabbed a knitting needle to use as a weapon—just in case—and jetted out the door herself, heading in the same direction as Rolex. The opposite of Fiona and the cemetery. The pair had aimed for the original office.

"Rolex," she called. "Where are you, baby? Momma's here.

You're safe. You can come out now. Rolex."

She veered from the cobblestone path, ducking under tree limbs and hopping over stones. Panic kept her in a frenzied state, tears stinging her eyes. She needed help. Trembling, gaze constantly scanning, she dialed Conrad. He answered on the third ring.

She wasted no time. "A woman broke into my house while I was gone. She had a key, Conrad. My brave Rolex chased her out the door, but now he's missing. Fiona is searching the property, and I'm headed to the old office but if I can't find him I'm going to burn the world down and dance in the flames."

"Jane!" Conrad barked. "Focus on me. Are you hurt?"

"Are you kidding? I'm *dying*, Conrad! My baby is missing."

"I mean physically, sweetheart. How are you physically? Are you bleeding?"

"Yes!" He'd called her sweetheart again, and it was wonderful and terrible, both perfectly and illy timed. "I'm bleeding *internally*. My heart is torn into a thousand pieces, and it's more than I can bear."

"We'll figure this out, I swear." His tone had gentled exponentially, allowing her to pick up background noises. Rustling. Keys jingling. Other people grunting. "I promise I'll stop at nothing to find your baby. But I do need *you* to stop what you're doing right now and listen to me. I'm on my way to you, but I'm an hour—half an hour out. Return to your house, bar the door, and dial Beau's number on the landline. He's nearby and can reach you faster. Do you understand? Keep me on the call and tell me every time you complete one of your tasks."

"Oh my gosh! Yes! You're right. Beau is close, so he can help the search. Thank you, Conrad. Bye." *Click.* Scanning here, there... Sunlight glared in every direction, few shadows offering relief.

GENA SHOWALTER & JILL MONROE

Sweat beaded on her brow as she rang her friend. As soon as Beau answered, she relayed what had happened.

Like Conrad, he jumped into action, heading her way. Also like Conrad, he told her to return home.

Jane hung up on him too and motored forward, shouting her cat's name. When she reached the top of the hill, the old office came into view and her breath caught. "Rolex!" At top speed, she dashed to the porch, where the mighty house panther rested on a shadow box, watching her approach with bored eyes. He even yawned.

"Oh, thank you, thank you, thank you!" She relinquished her weapon and dropped to her knees, gathering him close. A cheek nuzzle led to face-smothering kisses. Tears sprung anew, streaming down her cheeks. Her child was alive and well, and not in the clutches of some vicious cat killer.

Rolex squirmed for freedom, and she let him go. A quick phone call to Fiona ended the search. She phoned Conrad and explained the situation.

He muttered, "I want a look at that camera feed. While I'm there, I'll change the locks on your doors. If I leave without spanking you, it'll be a miracle." He hung up on her, and she smiled.

She'd just had the meltdown of the century, and he wasn't running for the hills. The guy had it bad for her. What if there was a slight chance he *didn't* fall prey to the curse? He was stronger than, well, anyone. His determination had no bounds. As he was proving, he didn't give up on *anything* without a fight. What if they could have something lasting?

Her tremors resumed as she called Fiona again just to say thank you. No one had better friends. Then she dialed Beau.

To her surprise, he offered complete understanding. "The momma bear found her cub. I'm glad. I'm also in your driveway."

Oh! "Fiona will let you in."

"No, she won't. I'm coming to get you. I'll escort you back to the house."

Did he think the masked intruder might be hiding nearby? What had the woman sought, anyway? Jane's possessions were priceless, but only in sentimental value.

Tension knotted her insides, and she rasped, "All right. Yes. I'll wait. Thank you." He was such a sweetheart.

The endearment echoed in her head, purred in Conrad's voice, and she melted down for another reason entirely. Oh yeah. He had it bad for her.

Fiona took off soon after she arrived, but Beau stayed. As promised, Conrad came over and replaced rusty, warped locks with new, shiny industrial-strength bolts at every entry point in the house. All the inside work now completed, just like the outside work. While she served snacks, the guys chatted like old friends, discussing their individual hobbies. To relax, Conrad restored classic cars. Beau built birdhouses and squirrel feeders. Both liked to work out, watch football and camp. Jane didn't mind roughing it upon occasion, if she got to stargaze.

As a little girl, she used to lie in Paradise Ladling, look up at the pinpricks of light set in an endless stretch of black, and chat with her relatives. No sight had ever rivaled the one painted by night. Until now.

She enjoyed watching the boys work together as a team. She'd first thought only Beau needed a friend, a buddy to hang and do guy stuff with. But seeing the pair side by side, hearing them call each other jerks and trashing the other's favorite sports teams, she realized Conrad needed the friendship every bit as much.

What she didn't appreciate? When the duo ganged up on her to declare her investigation days were over.

They could commiserate together when she proved them both wrong.

CHAPTER NINE

Arnold Hagen
Hole in One.
Plot 1024, Garden of Memories

*J*ane locked her car and jogged across the street toward the Aurelian Hills Gold Rush Museum, more determined than ever. Someone had endangered her precious cat, and that someone must be unearthed. Things were personal now.

The break-in *must* have a connection to Dr. Hotchkins's murder. Catch one, catch the other.

Would the intruder come back?

A shudder racked her. She didn't have to worry about Rolex while they were parted, at least. Those added bolts could hold a dragon.

The sun blazed, and she lamented her lack of a hat. Rolex had nibbled the tiniest little hole in her favorite straw, and she hadn't yet figured out how to repair it. Besides, any head-gear might make her stand out. Though new to investigating, she knew not to draw undue attention to herself, especially in a small town. She would draw enough attention already. So she'd opted for a plain T-shirt and jeans, hoping to blend in with other visitors.

She soared inside the building. A former county courthouse. Every schoolchild in Aurelian Hills visited the place at least once, and she couldn't help but relive the sense of giddy excitement she experienced that day. Clutching a sack lunch, Beau at her side. Oohing and awing over old tools.

A guide led a group of five past her, saying with a hushed tone, "Notice the red brick. Beautiful, right? Every piece is locally sourced, and if you squint really hard, you might even spot a trace of gold."

The same spiel Jane had heard at age six. And again at nine. Not once had she ever spied a hint of the stuff. Still, she'd always loved the federal-style building, with its white-painted shutters and tree-shaded sidewalk. An imposing yet charming picture.

Jane slowed when she reached the new and improved gold rush exhibit. She'd gotten mere glimpses at these crucial pages in Conrad's office. Now, she would have her own copies to study. And luck was on her side. After a month-long closing for repairs, the museum had reopened today for a limited time. Could there be a clearer sign that Jane was *supposed* to do this?

An attendant sitting at a rounded desk emblazoned with a golden peach greeted her with a smile. "Hello and welcome to the Gold Rush Museum, where you don't have to dig to find a treasure. If you're here for the morning tours, I'm sorry to say you've just missed the cutoff. You're free to do our self-guided one, however."

"Oh yes. Thank you," Jane replied with an eager nod.

"We only ask that you refrain from flash photography." The older woman handed her a pamphlet.

Well. She would just turn off her flash and take all the photos her heart desired. Problem solved.

After paying the entrance fee, she strode down a hallway lined with framed portraits of the courthouse and judges who'd once presided in the building. Beneath an arched doorway read a sign: *Welcome to the Nineteenth Century.*

Soft banjo music greeted her as she entered a large room. Detailed black-and-white murals depicting maps, settlers and mining equipment covered the walls. Backlit displays housed the tools of everyday life for the miners. Jugs, wooden spoons and the shallow pans used to sift gold flecks from the river rock.

On a mission, she headed for the journal displays. Hopefully, the staff hadn't retired anything after the renovation. She scanned the room until finding a special, five-sided glass enclosed table case.

Jane glanced from side to side. Alone. Good. She pulled out her notebook and catalogued some thoughts. Another look left. Right. She discreetly withdrew her phone. Flash off. Excellent.

She aimed her camera and tapped the screen without drawing notice to herself, then eyed the entrance. The coast remained clear. *Tap. Tap. Tap.* Emboldened, she moved on to the next display case. And the next. Jane visited presentation to presentation, capturing journal pages, legends of a once-secret society, maps and lists and scribbles and doodles and too many other things.

"Thanks," a woman called as she entered the smaller exhibit.

Wait. That woman. Red dress. Matching lipstick. Curvy figure. Jane remembered seeing her at Tiffany Hotchkins's house. Abigail Waynes-Kirkland. Did the socialite come here often?

Thankfully Jane had worn soft-soled shoes; she rushed to

a corner, wedged between two display cases and flattened herself against the wall to observe in secret. If only Conrad could see her now. *Nailing it!*

Abigail stalked from case to case, quickly looking over the contents before moving on. Then, at the first case where Jane had snapped a photo, the other woman paused and focused on a paper within, frowning. After glancing from side to side, Abigail popped out her phone and took a picture.

Hey, that was Jane's move. Also, you weren't supposed to use the flash. Abigail was gonna get them both thrown out. As soon as someone noticed the other woman's camera, someone else would no doubt tattle about Jane.

Why not initiate a conversation and distract her? If Jane unearthed some answers in the process, even better.

She snapped a quick photo of the other woman before easing from her hiding place and approaching her target. "Hello. Hi. Abigail, right? Do you remember me? I'm Jane."

They locked eyes for a moment, and Abigail blinked rapidly, offering a nervous laugh. "Jane. Yes." After another quick scan around the room. Growing serious, she latched onto Jane's wrist and tugged her into a shadow, whispering, "So you heard about the gold, too, I take it."

Jane's detective senses tingled. Did Abigail reference the fact that Dr. Hotchkins had enjoyed hunting the stuff? The fleur-de-lys? Or something more? Had he actually discovered some?

Better to play along and sort through the information later. "Oh yes. The gold," she whispered back, as if she too hoped to keep the secret. "I know everything. But how did *you* hear about it?"

"How else? Tiffany found Mark's notes."

Mark rather than Marcus. Very interesting. And yes, suspicious, suggesting a level of familiarity. Possibly intimacy. Not even Tiffany had referred to the man as Mark.

"Now it's your turn," Abigail said with a harsher undertone, tightening her grip on Jane's wrist. "I know Mark thought he'd turned up a reference to large nuggets hidden at your cemetery, but there was no mention of any gold reported on the news."

"Because there *isn't* any gold in my cemetery." Jane clicked her tongue. "Dr. Hotchkins was wrong. The coffins were looted years ago. A recorded fact."

"And coffins can't be refilled before they're reburied? What better spot to hide more gold than the place known to be picked bare? Grow up, Jane. You just want to keep everything for yourself."

Dr. Hots had truly believed new gold was hidden inside Jane's coffins? And Jane herself didn't know about it? "There's no gold," she reaffirmed, her tone flat. No one else had snuck over to try again, at least.

Hmm. Why had no one snuck over to try again? Not enough courage?

Better questions: How many people suspected gold lay buried on her property, and how many would grow desperate enough in the future to sneak over?

Jane flinched at the thought of treasure hunters crawling all over her land, messing up the grass and disturbing the peace.

"There's no gold," she repeated more forcefully.

Abigail searched her face, and after a moment, narrowed her eyes and released Jane's wrist. Backing away, palms up, she offered a brittle laugh. "Sure, sure. Whatever you say, Jane. Have a nice day." With that, she turned on her heel and stalked off, her high heels clicking and clacking, leaving Jane with a twisting stomach.

Her thoughts remained stuck. No way someone had buried new gold. Just no way. Right?

She took multiple photos from multiple angles of the

document Abigail had studied—the first one Jane would examine when she returned home. The urge to call Conrad surfaced, and she decided to go for it. He might complain about her involvement and command her to leave the museum, but he needed to hear these gold rumors.

Except the back of her neck prickled, and she straightened. Something felt weird. Jane darted her gaze. A group of museum guests entered the exhibit room, most engaged in a low conversation or focused on the displays. No one paid her any attention. No, not true. Everyone seemed to pay her too much attention, pretending not to notice her. Or she had an overactive imagination, and she needed to shift out of warp speed and into neutral.

Jane completed her mission and strolled from the building as casually as possible. She paused under the awning outside the entry doors. During the hour she'd spent inside, a storm front had rolled in, the sky now overcast. The coming rain electrified the air, her every inhalation scented moss and magnolia.

Something still felt weird, though. As if everyone around her suspected she carted around priceless gold pieces in need of stealing. Heart like a jackhammer, she glanced left. Right. Across Prospect Street to the fuller than usual parking lot. Nothing and no one out of place. But. Maybe she wouldn't head to her car just yet. Just in case.

Her nape continued to prickle as she motored down the sidewalk of the revitalized Downtown Market, passing shops and Aurelian Hills staples. The Goldfield Hotel and the Gilded Scissor Beauty Parlor. Old man Mr. Buckley sat on a rocker in front of his hobby shop, carving something from a slab of wood. Tammy and Tommy, the Williams twins, set up a chessboard under the Charter Oak, where Aurelian Hills was officially established. Some people waved as she passed;

others either didn't see her or looked past her. A few whispered, "That Cemetery Girl."

The feeling of being watched intensified. Jane threw another glance over her shoulder. Again, nothing out of the ordinary, but she quickened her steps. Never had she felt this way. She was tempted to phone Conrad, then Beau. But no. No, she was a grown woman, mature-ish even, sometimes, and she could handle anything on her own.

Nerves plagued her as she turned a corner and shot into Très Chic Consignment.

"Hi Jane," greeted Tawny, the owner of the shop. "No new hats since the last time you popped by."

Jane waved her hand. "That's okay. Maybe I'll discover a new, old favorite." She pretended to browse. When enough time had passed, her body calming, she eased back outside and retraced her steps, aiming for the museum. Okay. Better. Yes—nope. The prickles roared back.

An arm shot out from a shadowed corner, gripped her bicep, and yanked her into a hidden alcove between two buildings. A rotund man stood in front of her. Short, thinning almost fully gray hair. A nice nose. Square, shaved jaw. All familiar, but her recognition came too late. Fight or flight had kicked in, and Jane was already throwing a fist. Contact!

Stumbling back, Dr. Garcia roared and clutched his not-so-nice anymore nose.

"Sorry, sorry," she cried, pressing her aching hand over her racing heart. "Are you okay?"

Blood seeped through the cracks between his fingers. Dark eyes glazed with pain landed on her. "Ohh bwoke my nowse!"

"Well, yeah. You grabbed me. And followed me, I'm assuming. Why?" she demanded. She hadn't even called to make her second appointment yet.

Using his shirt sleeve, he cleaned his face as best he could.

His bicep flexed. He would definitely have an advantage in a fight.

Oh, crap. Would there be a fight?

"I needed to speak with you in private, and I suspect they've hidden cameras on your property," he said, his nasally voice layered with paranoia. "I'm sorry I frightened you. I promise I didn't mean to. I couldn't think of any other way to get you alone. I can't call you—I don't even have a cell phone. The GBH confiscated our equipment. Not just our phones, but our computers. The iPads. They subpoenaed everything the staff used to communicate with each other in the office or to post on message boards. Why do that? Who are they considering? I've never posted on a message board in my life. Has the agent said anything?"

No, the agent had not. Clearly, Conrad suspected a workplace romance gone bad, on the hunt for secret messages between lovers. Or meetings about gold. Did the message board tidbit add a whole new angle to the case?

Everyone in that medical clinic earned a new star at the top of her shady character list. Dr. Garcia, Caroline the PA and both nurses, with Emma maintaining a strong lead. "Special Agent Ryan hasn't mentioned your equipment, and he certainly hasn't named a suspect," she replied honestly. "Why would he? I grace his list, too."

"Yes, but everyone knows you're working with him, anyway. Emma mentioned you're dating him."

Everyone knew she was working *with* the GBH? And *dating* Conrad? And Emma had said this? Emma Miller, Jane's number one contender for murderer of the year? But how would Emma even know of Jane and Conrad's flirtation? They'd never ventured into town together. He'd come to the cemetery, or she'd gone to his office. They'd shared no other contact.

"Why does Emma think this?" she asked, genuinely baffled.

"She saw your notebook. You drew hearts around Special Agent Ryan's name and listed things to do on a date with him."

Her cheeks burned with embarrassment. Hastily drawn hearts and double date ideas did not equate to a relationship.

The doctor eased closer but stilled when she eased back. Holding up his hands in a gesture of innocence, he told her, "I didn't kill him. You must believe me. When I became a doctor, I took an oath. I would never harm anyone. *Never.* You have to believe me," he repeated.

"I don't understand why you think Conrad thinks—"

"We quarreled," he burst out, as if he couldn't bottle up the confession anymore. "The day Marcus died, we argued *badly.*" His shoulders rolled in, and his head lolled forward. The posture of a defeated man. "I called him terrible names. Cursed his very existence." Irritation joined the party, crackling in his voice. "But is that surprising? I'd just found out he was using our practice as his personal brothel. I'm not stupid. I know the legal risks. I begged to buy him out, but he refused."

So much to unpack. Motive galore. "I still don't understand why you think I can help."

Both the dejection and irritation faded, replaced by pure, undiluted fear. "I have an appointment to speak with Special Agent Ryan this afternoon. He called me two days ago and said I could drive to his office to answer his questions, or he could come and get me, whichever I preferred. Why be so harsh with me unless he thinks I'm the murderer?"

"He's harsh with everyone." That, she could claim without reservation. *Except to me. Sometimes.*

"Yes, but most people probably have alibis for the night of the murder. I was home, and I was alone." A bead of sweat dripped from his temple. "Maybe if you put in a good word for me and tell Special Agent Ryan you believe me? That you know I would never harm another living soul?"

A desperate man stood before her, and she sympathized. He only wanted to clear his name. She'd experienced the same rush of emotions when she became a suspect. Did she think he could kill Dr. Hotchkins? No. But also yes. She firmly believed everyone was capable of everything every day at every time.

"You don't have to worry, Dr. Garcia. The killer will be found, and the remaining will be exonerated. You only have to tell the truth."

"The truth?" he cried. "Don't be a fool, Jane. Innocent people go to prison all the time."

Was he innocent? Conrad hadn't mentioned the doctor during their meeting yesterday. An inadvertent omission or a purposeful one? Or did he not suspect Dr. Garcia of the crime, despite the shouting match?

"You aren't the only one with a reason to get rid of him, Dr. Garcia. Think of the many husbands he betrayed. The women he lied to. Be sure to tell Special Agent Ryan about them. Every detail." As he brightened, she asked, "How did you discover Dr. Hotchkins's, um, brothel?"

"I overheard the nurses discussing it. Emma was sobbing." He clutched his brow, as if the memory hurt his head. Or the pain from his nose was radiating. Maybe both. "She'd walked in on Marcus and a patient. He'd forgotten to lock the door, and they were...busy."

Emma again. And she'd just found out Dr. Hots had slept with another woman. A reason to rage. *Guiltier by the minute.*

A crack of thunder boomed. Both Dr. Garcia and Jane jumped.

He tossed a glance over his shoulder, as if he expected Conrad to leap into the alcove with a gun. "I better go." Amid another crack of thunder, he darted off, disappearing from view.

Jane hurried to her car, the dark sky opening up at the halfway point. By the time she leaped inside her sedan, her clothes were soaked and her teeth chattering. Her adrenaline crashed, the ignorable ache in her hand graduating into a noticeable throb. Motions clumsy, she started the car and cranked up the heat.

For several minutes, she debated the wisdom and foolishness of texting Conrad about what had just happened. In the end, she decided to take the advice she'd given Dr. Garcia and be honest.

She opened her first text thread with Conrad's number. Or rather, Agent Spice, as he was currently listed in her contact book. Ignoring the pain in her fingers, she typed, *Ran into Dr. Garcia (not my fault!) We chatted. He says he's innocent. I also bumped into Abigail Waynes-Kirkland at Gold Fever! She thinks there's gold buried in my cemetery. She heard it from Tiffany, who read Dr. Hotchkins's notes about it. Thoughts??????????*

A moment of pause, her finger hovering over the Send button. Should she? Shouldn't she? Too late. She pressed send.

Only seconds passed before the world's most exciting little bubbles appeared. Conrad was typing a response. And it must be a good one, because the bubbles stretched on and on and on.

Agent Spice: *Thanks.*

Thanks? Thanks! Ugh. How disappointingly official. And did he have to ignore her question altogether? Wait. New typing bubbles appeared, and she sat up straighter, bumping her sore knuckles into the steering wheel. She winced but didn't loosen her grip. What would he say this time?

Agent Spice: *Are you being safe? Legit gold or not, the mere suspicion puts you in danger.*

Aw. Her almost boyfriend—er, *date*—was concerned about her.

Jane: *Super safe!*

Proof: She might have broken Dr. Garcia's nose. With her fist. Self-defense? Yeah, she was practically a master. Oh, wait. She might need to mention the hurt nose. Conrad wasn't a half-bad detective, and he might notice the doctor's face at their meeting.

Jane typed and deleted. And typed. And retyped. Before she could hit send, her phone rang. She yelped, dropping the cell into her lap and scrambling to answer as Conrad's name flashed over the screen. "I assure you—" she began.

"You're typing too slow. Just tell me what's going on."

Now she had to verbalize everything? So cruel. "Um, so, quick detail, no big deal, because there's no way it's a crime since I did the right thing, given the circumstances and information at hand, so don't even think about arresting me, but I kind of punched Dr. Garcia in the face before we chatted."

Silence. She squirmed in her seat.

"Start from the beginning. I want to know every detail concerning both encounters. Waynes-Kirkland and Garcia." Tension crackled over the line as she explained. When she ended, he heaved a bone-weary sigh. "Do you have plans tonight?"

Imagining him at his desk, leaning back in his chair and scowling, she said, "Are you about to ask me on a real date? Because I might say yes, even though I really, really should say no. And not just because of the case." How was that for honesty?

"I'll take that as a no, you have no plans, so I'll be over at seven. I'll bring dinner, and you'll explain this mysterious reason to reject me. Dress comfortably. This isn't a date, but a training seminar. You'll be learning how to defend yourself on purpose."

"I accept your command/request, but don't bring food," she said, the words leaving her before she could think things through. "I'll cook."

CHAPTER TEN

SueAnn Pickens
No You Can't Have My Pecan Pie Recipe.
Plot 422, Garden of Memories

*R*ain accompanied Jane the entire fifteen-minute drive to the grocery store, where she purchased ingredients to create a delightful meal for Conrad. Just something simple, like she used to cook with Grandma Lily. Chicken-fried steak and scratch gravy. Black-eyed peas. All the greens. Mashed potatoes. Homemade rolls. Cornbread, as well as stuffing. Corn. Sweet potatoes.

Since she didn't know what kind of pie he preferred, she should probably bake an array. Chess. Pecan. Peach. A cherry cobbler, if she had time. Yeah, she'd definitely have time.

The rain continued to fall until five seconds after she raced inside the house, soaked anew. Rolex greeted her with a soft meow. He perched on top of the couch so she could adore him. After the appropriate amount of fawning, he sauntered away and she wandered into the kitchen. She made herself a peanut butter and jelly sandwich and decided not to phone the clinic and schedule an appointment with Caroline and Emma.

Why give Emma a heads-up? Instead, Jane could pose as a walk-in. A surprise. While there, she would try not to throw up in her mouth each time she wondered how many patients Dr. Hots had banged on the table.

After unloading her groceries and donning an apron, she uploaded today's photos onto her laptop, then grabbed her investigation notepad and a pen to log her thoughts.

Knowing how to prepare every dish by route, she studied the images, noting the scribbles she both could and couldn't decipher, names and dates, symbols, maps and coordinates. Writing as she worked, alternating between whisking and dipping and peeling. Hidden in the photos she'd taken at the exhibit lay the explanation for Dr. Hotchkins's belief that gold filled some of her caskets.

Hmm. Something niggled in the back of her mind. She slid her gaze over everything she'd found worthy enough to be logged in her notebook, hoping an idea would catch—there. The fleur-de-lys symbol continued to draw her attention. What looked like the serious side of a sword and two curved lines forming the hilt.

Was she missing something? According to Conrad, the image was linked to the gold. But how? How?

Jane slid the last pie in the oven, set the timer, then checked the different camera streams. Nothing out of the ordinary. Excellent. An hour till the pie baked and two hours until Conrad's arrival. Enough time for paperwork, light cleaning and a shower.

As she waited, she compiled her outstanding bills and balanced the accounts, lamenting the lack of extra funds. A little gold would not be amiss right now. Oh, the things she could update at the cemetery. The cottage. The wages she could pay Beau!

The oven's timer buzzed. She hurried over to pull the pie from the oven, then tidied the kitchen. Finally, with the dishes covered and the table set, she showered. Once dry, she donned a tank top, shorts and tennis shoes, her best workout clothes.

Hair up or down? What would Conrad prefer? Nope. His opinion didn't matter. Up.

Oh! She'd forgotten to prepare a fresh batch of sweet tea. Where the heck were her manners?

Back to the kitchen she went, tying an apron around her waist. Rolex observed from the counter as Jane boiled water, dipped tea bags and mixed cup after cup of sugar. She had just finished stirring when the doorbell rang. Nervousness and excitement collided.

The excitement struck her as pure foolishness. This wasn't a date. He had specifically said so. Yes, Conrad had caught feelings for her. Yes, she debated the merits of risking the wrath of the Ladling curse. Yes, she had already forgotten where she'd been going with this. He was here!

She smoothed the ruffle on her apron and made her way to the door, Rolex on her heels. A twist of the knob, a creak of hinges, and a surprising sight greeted her, the fluttering worsening. Conrad, standing next to Beau. The dark-haired bruiser and the blond Viking.

Rolex hissed at one, then the other. *Good kitty.*

Conrad looked incredible in a fitted T-shirt and worn jeans, his tattooed forearms on display. She wanted to study every image in great detail but kept her gaze up. No reason to make him feel like a piece of meat yet.

Beau wore a T-shirt and shorts, as if he'd come straight from the gym. Muscles abounded.

"Don't mind me. I'll be installing an alarm system from wall to wall, floor to ceiling," Beau said. Then he nodded and strode inside, his delicious pine-and-soap scent a perfect complement to the aroma wafting from the kitchen. A duffel bag hung from his hand.

"Not unless I get a bill first," she called. "Which you can give me at dinner. Which you are eating with us, so don't even consider saying no." She motioned Conrad inside. "You told him about Dr. Garcia, I take it?"

"I did not. I informed him of the gold. As he is your security guard, I believed he needed to be in the know. I made a judgment call. The real question is, why didn't *you* tell him?"

Because she owed Beau so much already, their friendship was lopsided. He did everything, and she did nothing. She wasn't used to having a close ally nearby and feared she might drive him away. Fiona didn't count because Fiona was family. For the bulk of Jane's twenty-six years, she'd spent more time with the dead than the living. "I won't take advantage of our relationship."

"When it involves safety, scales cease to matter," Conrad told her as he entered the house. "Why is there a scale between you and Beau in the first place?" He backed her up, shutting and locking the door without ever looking away. "Until *I* catch the killer, let Beau help you every way he can. Okay?"

He eased back, resting against the entrance. Giving her a choice: stay put or move closer. She moved closer. Just a little bit. Just to inhale all that cedar and spice.

Then his words registered. "I know why Beau decided he liked you," she grumbled. "What flipped the switch from animal-kingdom rules to bro code for *you*?"

He shrugged his broad shoulders. "Do you really want to discuss it?" His gaze dropped to her lips before flipping up. "Or would you rather hear my thoughts about you instead?"

Their gazes held—and sizzled. She lost her breath.

"I don't need you to tell me. I can guess," she rasped. "Too curious. Too superstitious about curses. And fun." He had smiled at her sometimes. "Am I right? I'm right, aren't I?"

"Sorry, but I deem my impressions of you classified until the case closes." Did she detect a note of affection? Dark eyes playful, he reached around her to untie the apron, and suddenly she felt defenseless, as if she'd lost her shield. "The food smells amazing. Let's eat."

Seriously? "You're gonna end the conversation like that?"

He winked and walked on. Dang him. Jane darted in front of him, leading the way to the dining room, where Beau was setting up shop on the yellow-laminate counter that divided the kitchen from the dining room. Why wasn't Rolex watching him, hissing with displeasure?

Hey, where was her precious, most treasured companion? After the Incident, she was taking no chances. Gearing up to panic, she scanned—oh, thank goodness. Air seeped from her lungs, tense muscles easing. Rolex had returned to perch on the table. He glared at both men as if he'd already plotted their murders in eighteen different ways. How almost gentle of him. He must be acclimating to having guests.

"Sit, sit," she said, motioning the boys to the chairs. She rushed to the china cabinet to collect another plate, then brought out the first dish. Then the next. And the next. Just the way Grandma Lily used to serve when they entertained.

Proper manners are always in style, my darling.

"I've seen nothing like this," Conrad rasped, his eyes wide as he took in the assortment.

Uh-oh. Was "this" a good thing or bad thing? Beau bore a similar expression of astonishment.

"Are you expecting other guests?" her friend asked, his brow wrinkled.

"Nope. Just us. Why?" She claimed the chair between the two men and thrilled as they both filled their plates. "Oh, make sure to save room for dessert. I baked your favorite pie."

Conrad canted his head at her. His official detective power pose. He'd decided there was a mystery to be solved. "I'm curious. What is my favorite pie?"

"I don't know," she quipped. "We'll find out together."

A megawatt smile bloomed, lighting his entire face. Jane felt her cheeks flush and her heart race.

Beau cleared his throat and adjusted his collar. "I get that you guys are having a moment, but I'm starved. Mind if I dive in?" He rubbed his hands together.

Jane laughed and motioned to the food. "Please do." As she filled her plate, Conrad noticed the bruises on her hand and stiffened.

He reached out and cupped his fingers under hers, lifting her battered knuckles to study them in the light. His features darkened. She nibbled on her bottom lip, expecting a rebuke. Instead, he flipped up his gaze and offered her a proud smile. "You blackened both his eyes. Good job." After lightly tracing the pad of his thumb over her knuckles, he released her.

She bit back a whimper. "Is that better or worse than breaking his nose?"

"You did both. A broken nose caused the black eyes. And they are equal."

Well. You learn something new every day. "My first time throwing a punch, and I hit the bull's eye."

"If someone ever grabs you again, go for their throat and run away screaming," Beau said with a nod. "You *will* run away screaming, won't you, Jane?"

"As fast as your feet can carry you," Conrad added after sipping his tea. "Scream fire if you must."

The food in her stomach turned to lead. "You guys expect more trouble, don't you?"

Conrad set down his fork to rub the back of his neck. "I

have an agent monitoring the Headliner, and as of this after-noon eleven subjects have mentioned the possibility of finding gold in your cemetery. Those eleven will tell others. Those people will spread the word further. At some point, someone will sneak onto your property to find out the truth."

"Whatever day it is, whatever time, I want you to call me at even the hint of a trespasser." Beau's green eyes were fierce. "I mean it."

Jane nodded, her thoughts whirling. Was there or wasn't there gold in her cemetery?

They finished the meal, and both men offered to clean up. Though she refused—Grandma Lily never allowed guests in the kitchen—they helped her, anyway.

"Beau has a lot to do, and I have a lot to teach you," Conrad said when the last dish was put away. "We should get started."

As Beau installed the alarms throughout the house, the agent trained Jane by porch light in the backyard. A wide space with lush grass and graceful willows. Lighting bugs flashed, the scent of magnolia heavier than usual. Stars glit-tered like diamonds scattered over black velvet. A sultry evening with a powerful man.

He was a hands-on trainer, a bit barky, and he showed no mercy, but she loved every minute. He taught her how to fight as dirty and nasty as possible. Best move by far? The Testicle Relocator.

He kept things all business, and his serious demeanor never wavered. Until she did an impression of him, and he laughed outright. The rusty sound broke and delighted her heart in unison.

"You're a natural," he told her, the praise going straight to her head.

Beau finished soon after and took off. Conrad lingered a

bit longer. He dusted his knuckles along her jawline before heading to his car with a wink and a smile. "Try not to miss me too much."

Impossible. "Don't die on your way home," she called with a wave, and he laughed outright.

Jane was still smiling as she prepared for bed. What a wonderful night.

As she laid her head upon her pillow, the image she'd found so familiar resurfaced in her mind, and she gasped, jolting upright. Finally! She knew what had niggled at her about the fleur-de-lys. Add a circle to the bottom and a circle with a dot in the center and *boom*, you had the symbol for the (alleged) Order of Seven. A long-ago gold-worshipping secret society. The same symbol her ancestors had carved in the gold-bearing coffins. The very symbol marked in one of the journals on display at the museum.

There it was. The connection. But was it a decoy or the real deal? Would she find gold in some of her coffins? In any of the other marked caskets?

After the graves were looted, her ancestors logged details describing every detail about every plot and coffin. Jane knew some of their old notes mentioned the Order of Seven symbol.

She scrambled out of bed, one thought rolling into another. She'd seen the pattern on the unearthed casket as well as a photo at the museum. The same photo Abigail had studied—the grave of Silas Ladling.

I'm on to something. I know it! Jane needed a partner, and there was only one person she trusted to do the job and not arrest her.

She snatched up her cell phone and teed up his number.

He answered on the first ring, tension icing his voice. "What's wrong?"

"Nothing. You wanna dig up a grave?"

CHAPTER ELEVEN

Adam Daniels
In The Hole On This Deal.
Plot 681, Garden of Memories

"*W*hy are we doing this again?" Beau shoveled a mound of dirt from inside a pit.

Jane had hung paper lanterns throughout the area, golden light keeping her companion illuminated.

Midnight had come and gone, insects serenading them with a gentle song as a magnolia scented breeze brushed warm air over her exposed skin. "Because we can." Jane perched atop a headstone, the perfect spot to see inside the pit. She wore a tank top, jeans and her sturdiest work boots. "Why did you agree?"

"I knew you'd come out here on your own if I didn't."

"Smart."

Dirt smeared his sweat-glistened skin. Everywhere from his brow to the beginnings of a golden happy trail, visible above the waist of his jeans. He'd removed his shirt an hour ago, and she couldn't help but notice he was a seriously beautiful man. He was also kind beyond imagining. Caring. A little—or a lot—haunted. Still not great at smiling. But at least he was relaxing more.

Mental note: *Call Eunice and/or Ana about that double date!*

"Let me rephrase. Why am *I* doing this?" he grumbled, hoisting another scoop of dirt out of the hole, his well-defined biceps straining. "This is your idea. You should be the one huffing and puffing."

She offered him the same expression often displayed to Jane herself. Amused indulgence. The equivalent of a pat on the head. "But Beau," she said with an exaggerated pout, "all of my digging equipment stopped working ages ago. Since there are to be no more burials, I decided not to waste money fixing everything. Now I rely on my trusty shovel. I only found one shovel."

He snorted. "Yes, but I happen to know you have three others. You hid them, didn't you?" He plunged the blade in the earth again, all kinds of muscles rippling. *Thunk.*

Beau stilled. Their gazes met.

Breathless with excitement, she asked, "Does that mean what I think it means?"

"Oh yeah." He shoveled faster to reveal the upper part of a seriously old casket. "We hit pay dirt."

She hopped down and crouched, the lantern casting brighter rays into the depths of the hole. Carved in the center of the lid? The Order of Seven symbol, as noted by her ancestor.

A rush of adrenaline flooded her veins. "I'm joining you in the pit. This is happening, so don't try to stop me." Jane secured the ladder she'd placed at the ready and climbed down, bringing the lantern with her. She wiped the remaining layer of dirt from the casket's surface.

Beau continued digging around the edges to provide a fingerhold. "Again, I gotta ask. You're sure this is legal?"

On her knees, she propped her hands on her hips. "Look at you, all concerned about the law. I mean, it's about as legal as it's gonna get without a court order. This grave belongs to Silas Ladling, the first resident of Garden of Memories. As his heir, I grant permission for this exhumation. As the groundskeeper, I offer no protests to said permission. See? *Extra* legal."

He flashed her a dubious look but reached for the crowbar anyway. Friends were awesome. The aged wood creaked as he pried open the seal. Beau's complexion suddenly took on a greenish hue, and it had nothing to do with the lighting.

"That smell," he choked.

"Don't be silly. The body is too old to have a smell. No, what you're smelling is the scent of a new curse being unleashed upon an unsuspecting world. I kid, I kid."

He narrowed his eyes. "Have you always been this way?" His nose wrinkled as the last nail gave and they ~~broke into~~ popped open the lid. "I swear I'm inhaling death itself." He shuddered and gagged.

A smile spread. Sometimes she forgot how squeamish other people got around gravestones and caskets and dead bodies. She gave her big tough guy's muscly arm a gentle squeeze. "Be honest. You believe you've unleashed a vengeful ghost who will forever haunt you."

"I didn't. But I do now," he griped.

"Don't worry. I'll protect you from most likely nonexistent entities. In the meantime, just breathe through your mouth. In and out. Good, that's good."

Her own breath hitched in anticipation as she returned her attention to the casket. This might be the most exciting development since she'd joined the investigation team. Real answers about Dr. Hot's death, legends, secret symbols and buried gold could be hers in mere seconds.

Her fingers trembled as she lifted the lid.

For over a hundred years, this casket had remained buried, bothered only by time, the elements and once, those looters. Was Abigail right? Had someone hidden more gold before the second burial? The wood protested with a splintering groan as the top separated from the bottom.

Beau kept his gaze on the star-studded sky above them, no doubt plotting his escape route.

With a final mournful sound, the burial box grudgingly revealed its secrets. "This is it," she said, goose bumps spreading over her arms as she adjusted the lamp. She'd never felt so amped for a moment.

Light chased the shadows from the coffin's aged interior.

"Well." Her shoulders rolled in. "Empty."

"Someone stole the body?" Beau dropped his gaze, only to zoom it back to the sky. He covered his mouth, gagging once again, and a giggle escaped her. Glaring her way, he barked, "You said the thing was empty but it's filled with bones."

"I meant there's no gold." Which meant, what? That she was right and the new rumors about gold proved to be nothing more than speculation? That she should focus on the romance angle? Namely Emma Miller?

"Let's get out of here," Beau said, closing the lid. "I want to shower with scalding water and steel wool. I think the smell of rot has infused into my skin."

"Tsk, tsk. Such a silly rabbit." She remained in place. "My ancestor was barely a body."

"Exactly!" He wagged a finger at her. "Did you have this mean streak as a little girl?"

"Yes. Now be a good boy and look away again. I'm not done collecting my evidence." She opened the lid, the hinges groaning louder than before.

Beau muffled a cough, and she laughed.

"I'll be quick, I promise," she assured him. "I just need to take a few pictures to post on the Headliner. Don't worry. I won't show anything I shouldn't."

"All of it is something you shouldn't show. Despite your assurances to the contrary, we broke several laws, and you're about to confess to the world. You understand this, yes?"

She angled her camera this way and that, snapping photo after photo. "How did I not know you were such a worrywart?"

He reared back. "I am not a worrywart."

"You so are."

Now he pursed his lips. "If you're going to make me wait, you might as well remind me about the Aurelian Hills gold rush. I only lived in the area a little while, and I recall little about the history here. How did the gold get into the caskets? The first time."

Did he need a distraction? As she took photos, she told him, "From what I've read, the town had a thief in its midst back then. Someone willing to steal the gold found by others. My ancestor buried his nuggets with the new arrivals for safekeeping, thinking to wait until the heat died down. But then he died."

"Of course he did." He moved to the ladder and waved her over. "All right. That's all I can stand. I'll help you refill the hole in the morning, but we're done for the night. It's late, and I'm tired."

And he had a drive ahead. "Where are you living, exactly?"

"In a motel just outside of town."

What! A motel when she had a perfectly amazing guest room? For shame! "Why don't you stay here tonight? The guest bedroom has a private bathroom. I'll even provide clean clothes. Grandma Lily kept some of my grandpa's things after he died. They're dated and probably, uh, a teensy bit small for you, but I'll make up for it with a breakfast feast." He'd come all this way and done so much to aid her. She wanted to do something nice for him, too.

"I liked the motel," he said. "But I'll stay tonight because I don't like the thought of you out here alone with those rumors about gold floating around. No need to break out your grandfather's clothes. I always keep a go bag in my truck. It has everything I need."

A go bag? For one-night stands? Or getting out of town fast? The thought of losing him choked her up.

Silent, she followed him up the ladder and snapped a few photos of the hole and gravestone from several angles.

Beau let her work up here without complaint, but he did shift his weight from foot to foot, eager to escape. Her big, strong friend and his corpse phobia. Yep. Adorable.

Inside the house, she, Beau and Rolex double checked the locks, windows and perimeter. She took a shower to wash off the grime, dressed in full coverage pajamas and headed for the kitchen, while chatting softly with Rolex too amped to sleep.

The guest room door was closed, the lights out. Had Beau already drifted off? An idea struck.

She hurried to compile an itemized list of everything he'd done for her and the money she owed him, then slipped the paper under his door. If he wouldn't give her a bill, she'd give him an IOU.

After making a cup of tea, she settled in Grandma Lily's favorite overstuffed recliner and withdrew her phone from her pocket. With the sweetest purrs, Rolex rested on the arm of the chair and drifted to sleep.

She turned the cell to silent, then edited the photos she'd taken, blurring the body before uploading the best images to the Headliner. To her surprise, the entire process took less than half an hour.

See? No gold at Garden of Memories. RIP Silas Ladling.

She set her phone aside and leaned back, teacup in hand. Warm, chamomile-scented steam misted her face. How long before Conrad found out what she'd done? He'd mentioned he kept the Headliner group under surveillance. Surely the people keeping vigil took nighttime breaks? A quick glance at the clock. 4:03 a.m. Or morning breaks.

She bet Conrad contacted her first thing in the morning. Eight, maybe. Or even seven. A ripple of excitement shot down her spine. No doubt he would—

Her phone vibrated, and she gasped. Less than five minutes? *Are you kidding me?*

"You dug up a body?" he demanded without preamble. "With help from a certain someone, I'm sure."

"Why isn't your first guess looters, since everyone in town has heard rumors about the gold?" she asked him quietly, being respectful of Beau's nearness, and involvement. "I might have taken photos of their crime. In fact, I might be calling a certain special agent right now to report said crime. But however it happened, I think we can both agree it was my billion-year-old relative, my decision."

A soft growl filled the line. "We wanted to douse the flames of interest in the cemetery, not to fan them."

His gravelly voice tickled her ears. "The coffin had no gold. Consider the flames doused. You're welcome, by the way. You can repay me by opening up my cemetery and removing the police tape." It hadn't bothered her before, but for some reason, it bothered her now.

"First, I planned to call you in the morning and tell you the cemetery is cleared for visitors. Second, check out your text messages. I've sent you several screenshots. Comments from your post."

Uh-oh. He'd grated those words with more force than before.

Jane held her phone in front of her face and opened the

new messages from Conrad. Though most of the towns-people were asleep, two night owls had already replied.

Believe Cemetery Girl's staged picture? Try again. Stated by John Langston, a guy she'd gone to high school with. A bona fide conspiracy theorist, so big deal.

You obviously removed the gold before taking those photos. Posted by the mayor.

Okay, that one came with a sting. Her fingers tightened around the phone as she returned the device to her ear. "So that didn't go exactly as planned. How do I prove there's no gold here?"

His heavy sigh crackled over the line before he grumbled, "I know that tone. It means you're already plotting something else. Stop it. Stop it right this second."

Too late. Ideas rolled through her mind. "I think I need to launch a sting operation."

"No," he stated simply. "No sting operation, Jane."

"I'll host a tour, like I've done countless times in the past. Business as usual. Except I'll charge double. Triple! Prices so exorbitant they weed out the merely curious. Only people invested in the case or the gold will pay. And you can't forbid this, because the cemetery is still cleared for business, yes? Mourners gotta mourn, Conrad."

"Yes. You are still cleared to open your business." He'd graduated from demanding to hissing. "What do you hope to learn from this?"

Easy. "Who's interested in the gold or the murder, as previously stated. Who's interested in the gold, period. If someone attempts to snag the murder weapon. Finally ending the mystery about gold for everyone in town, making myself and my cat safer. Gaining a chance to look my home intruder in the eye. Revenge. Finding out if there's someone paranoid enough to double check no evidence was left behind. Shall I go on?"

"How do you make sense?" He heaved another sigh. "I can't believe I'm doing this. Come to my office first thing in the morning. Eight sharp. If I can't stop your tour, I'll help you as much as I can."

He would? Really? "Thank you, Conrad. Thank you, thank you, thank you."

"Goodnight, Jane." But he didn't hang up. Not yet.

"Something else you wanna say, Conrad?" she said, and chewed on her bottom lip. Had she sounded as needy to him as she'd sounded to herself? In that moment, the Ladling curse meant nothing to her. She only wanted more of this man.

Another sigh. "I'm really glad I met you, sweetheart."

Sweetheart again. Her chest clenched, a stronger squeeze than ever before. Tomorrow, the curse could matter again. For tonight? "I'm glad I met you too."

They hung up, then, and she and Rolex crawled into bed. She tried to fall asleep, but her mind remained too active, running through the information, pairing different clues together. By six, she gave up and meandered into the kitchen, ready to start breakfast for Beau.

A note rested on the table alongside the shredded remains of her IOU.

We're friends. You owe me nothing. I'll stop by later, and you can tell me about your meeting with Conrad. B

So the two had already chatted? Men sucked. They were so freaking annoying. And so, so pretty. But mostly annoying. She couldn't exactly prepare herself a feast, now, could she? Instead, she had to settle for whole grain.

Forget it. She had time to kill before making the hour-long drive to the city. Why not have pancakes. Except, they weren't Fiona's pancakes.

Back to whole grain.

CHAPTER TWELVE

Brian McGowan
I Told You That Tasted Funny.
Plot 77, Garden of Memories

*J*ane stood behind a big potted plant in the lobby of Georgia Bureau of Homicide headquarters, phone pressed to her ear, writing in her note-book and hiding from the receptionist as she finished her call with Fiona. A big sign had been taped to the desk: NO CELL PHONES PAST THIS POINT.

Half rebellious, half afraid of being ticketed for a cell phone violation, she whispered, "Repeat what you just told me, word for word. Leave nothing out. I think I'm missing some details."

Her friend sighed. "Why don't I stick to the highlights? An hour ago, a distraught Emma Miller knocked on my door. She said she got a call from someone on her way to work, and they told her I'd been asking questions about her. She demanded to know why. *I* demanded to know why she cared, and she stomped away."

A quick double check. Okay, yes. Jane had logged the pertinent details. "That woman is *so* guilty."

"Agreed. The answer doesn't always need to be complicated. That's what I always say, anyway." A pause. "Are you about to see Conrad?" Fiona asked, her dead-serious tone replaced by amusement.

"In a matter of minutes." She swiped her tongue over her lips. "In fact, I should go. Don't want to be late."

They hung up, and she stashed her phone but kept her trusty notebook and a pen in hand.

Jane slipped from her spot behind the plant and moved to the reception desk. Nervousness and excitement battled for domination in the arena of her mind. Soon, she would kick off Operation Killer Bait.

Mission Make the Cat Nabber Pay?

Ghost Tour Takedown?

Burial Bust?

Or maybe Gold Collar, the longshot of the batch?

Which codename would Conrad prefer? Or had he already selected one?

After she showed the receptionist her ID, she received a visitor's badge and a wave toward the correct path.

A woman of importance, Jane held her head high, and okay, yes, she had a little hop in her step as she strolled the distance. She'd chosen a floral fit and flare with spaghetti straps that Grandma Lily had made for her. A special occasion dress. What was more special than planning to nab a killer who might also dabble in breaking and entering?

Finding Conrad's door open, she sailed inside. He leaned against the corner of his desk, his arms crossed over his chest. Had he been waiting (eagerly) for her?

Different parts of her fluttered. He looked good. Better than good. Dark hair in disarray, whiskey eyes more intoxicating than ever as they slid over her. A new five o'clock shadow dusted his jaw. Too distracted to shave this morning?

He'd already removed his jacket, unbuttoned the top two buttons of his shirt, and rolled up his sleeves. The tattoos drew her gaze. She'd never let herself study them before. Today, she thought, why not? The most adorable stick figures and rainbows and weirdly shaped animals decorated his skin. The images reminded her of a child's drawings. Were they?

Who had drawn them? What did the images mean to him?

"You're late," he said, his rich voice raising goose bumps along her arms.

Uh… "How?" She glanced at the clock hanging on his back wall. "I'm two minutes early."

"Yes, but ten minutes early is the new on time, which makes you exactly eight minutes tardy." He straightened and stalked to his chair. "We should get started."

Jane rolled her eyes. "We should indeed." She plopped into a chair, all but bouncing on the cushion.

"You look beautiful, by the way." He extended the compliment while searing her with his gaze.

No longer an aloof special agent, Conrad made her toes curl. The tempting man who taught her self-defense, rushed to her cat's rescue, called her sweetheart, and robbed her of breath.

She offered him a shy smile. Wait. Her? Shy? And *beautiful?* "Thank you." Before she threw herself at him, she cleared her throat and flipped through the pages of her notepad as casually as possible. As if she received such overwhelming compliments every day.

"All right." He braced, as if expecting some kind of blow. "Let's get to business. The tour. You know we have the camera on Muffin's marker. It is monitored twenty-four seven. There's no *need* for a tour."

"Actually, there is. Your camera has caught a big, fat nothing, I bet."

He scowled. Translation: *I hate when you're right, Jane.*

Hey. Speaking of Muffin. "What happened with the crowbar?"

"It is indeed the murder weapon."

A grin spread. "It is? I did it, then? I found the most crucial piece of evidence in the entire case?"

He might have fought a smile. "The metal is splattered with Dr. Hotchkins's blood and covered with his fingerprints."

Someone pat her on the back. Jane was *made* for investigative work. "Any other fingerprints?"

"None." He gripped a pen and tapped the edge against his desk. "I think I've made it clear I don't want you to do the tour, Jane."

"You have, yes, but it always sounds like a *you* problem," she said, batting her lashes at him.

He pursed his lips. "But," he continued as if she hadn't spoken, "I can't stop you from doing it. If you insist on putting yourself in the line of danger, I will insist on doing something as well."

Something to protect her? What a sweet thing to—

"I'll use you to draw the killer out," he said, and she deflated a little. "I think anything out of the ordinary will draw undue suspicion." He slid a piece of paper across the desk. A pamphlet she'd once handed out to drum up business for her tours. "Scheduling a tour like this fits your profile."

"Like this? A plain ole tour with no theme?" Her shoulders slumped. She'd hoped to do something different. Adventurous. "Where's the drama? Everyone loves drama. Shouldn't I give the people what they want?"

"We don't care about what the people want," he reminded her. "We care about a killer. When should we ever cater to a killer?"

"Never," she grumbled.

"Good girl. Now," he continued, "you can make it seem like you're capitalizing on the unsolved murder or claim you can prove there's no hidden gold. Considering what you posted to the Headliner last night, the latter is the most believable. You've gotten over fifty comments, each one accusing you of being a liar."

She didn't miss the censure in his tone and winced. "My bad." Yeah, she'd gone over every comment before heading to the city. Apparently only Fiona and Beau believed her. "I'll go with a gold theme."

His fingers twitched on the arms of his chair at the same time a muscle jumped in his jaw. "I will attend, of course, and I will—"

"No! Are you kidding? The killer won't come if a GBH agent is there."

"Nevertheless. I'll be buying a ticket." He offered her a smug smile. "As a paying customer, I'll have every right to stand by your side, keeping you safe."

So he would be protecting her. Just as sweet as she'd originally thought. No, more so. But also beyond aggravating. "Beau will be there." Thinking out loud, she said, "No one will try anything with him around. He's playing the part of groundskeeper."

"Then I'll be playing the part of Conrad, the groundskeeper's helper. And you're right. Many will recognize me. I want them to."

Argh! He wasn't backing down. He knew everyone would recognize him, no matter what he wore. But she was feeling a little bit petty now. "I can't wait to see you in the costume I plan to prepare for you."

"The groundskeeper's helper doesn't require a costume."

"He's getting one anyway," she said and *humphed*. "I'm putting a rush on this tour. Scheduling it for this weekend. You probably have plans—"

"I'll be there." Sizzling brown eyes dared her to try and stop him.

The way he was looking at her right now... Special Agent Conrad Ryan clearly had plans for her once the case closed. *Do not shiver. Don't you dare!*

"Fine," she said, hating how breathless she sounded. "Come as a paying guest. You'll not be getting a discount, so don't ask. Actually, your ticket has an out-of-town processing fee. Add a hundred dollars to it."

He snorted. "Tell me who you expect to show up."

She flipped through the pages of her notebook until she reached a dog-eared page in back—her most up-to-date list of suspects. "Emma Miller is my number one. Before the murder, she found out Dr. Hots was sleeping with other women. Dr. Garcia caught her crying. Of course, he's on my list as well. As well as Caroline Whittington and everyone else at the clinic. And their significant others."

"Yes, but who's second on your list?"

So many! Basically a who's who of Aurelian Hills. But, if she *had* to pick from the three-dozen or so remaining names, she'd go with... "Abigail Waynes-Kirkland."

His head canted to the side as he regarded her more intently. "Why her?"

The infamous tilt. She almost grinned. She'd definitely intrigued him. Was he surprised by the name itself, or by that Jane considered the woman a suspect? "She was close to the doctor. At the wake she seemed bitter about his affairs. She visited *Gold Fever!* and she refers to Marcus as Mark."

"Which is suspicious why?"

"She's the only one who uses such familiarity. They might

have had an affair." But back to the gold. "Have you heard of the Order of Seven?"

A pause. Then, "It may have come up in a meeting."

"Well, allow me to captivate your imagination with what I know about it. I did some digging." Both literally and figuratively. "The Order of Seven was a secret society formed during the gold rush. An urban legend usually shared among teenagers. At the exhibit, Abigail studied one paper exclusively. A page referencing the Order. Here, I'll text you the photos I took of her and the page when I visited the museum against your wishes. It's the same base symbol that was spray-painted all over town." Once found, she sent him a series of images.

The more his phone dinged with the shared jpegs, the more irritation he projected. "Why am I just now seeing these photos?"

"I didn't know if the lead would pan out. Brilliant pun intended."

He appeared far from amused. "I want a copy of any documents you have."

"Sure. Because you requested so sweetly." *Anyway.* "Abigail knew all about the new gold supposedly stashed in my cemetery, and she zeroed in on the clearest shot of the Order of Seven symbol. The same symbol is carved into the caskets of Rhonda Burgundy and Silas Ladling."

She scooted to the edge of her seat, getting into her story. "Silas Ladling's son was rumored to be a member of the Order. But he took a devastating financial hit when our mines petered out and gold was discovered in California. In a matter of weeks, Aurelian Hills lost half its population, businesses suddenly without paying customers."

"And you think, what? That the Order is active again, the members searching for hidden gold?"

"Not necessarily. But Dr. Hotchkins did dabble in hunting

gold. You said so yourself. What if he had a partner who found some—outside my land—and didn't want to share?" It was an angle she hadn't fully explored because she'd gotten stuck on the doctor's affairs. An angle she hadn't abandoned. "To be honest, though, my gut is telling me a scorned lover did the deed." As Conrad had said, the motive for murder was usually love or money.

"Almost eighty percent of killers are male," he informed her. "That favors the gold angle."

"Wow. A woman is as capable and likely of committing a murder as a man. We're just better at hiding it." She tried to hide how she relished competing verbally with him. Who was wrong about the murder's motive, and who would have eternal bragging rights?

He leaned back in his chair, locking his fingers behind his head. The glitter of amusement had returned to his irises. "That's a brave thing for a former suspect to say to an officer of the law during an ongoing investigation."

"When did I become a *former* suspect?"

He flicked his tongue over an incisor before admitting, "When you looked at me with those big blue eyes."

Gah! He needed to shut his sexy mouth. Already Jane feared melting into a puddle of goo. "Am I a former suspect who now qualifies for a tour of the crime lab?"

The corners of his mouth twitched. "Your thought process fascinates me, but no. No tour. However, when this is over, I'll exchange a visit of the building for a visit of your mind. I'm taking a vacation and sitting down with you. I will ask questions, and you will answer. For days. We'll do other things, too, but one way or another, I will learn all of your secrets."

Mind blown. Her eyes widened, and her breath caught, speech impossible for a moment.

His amusement only intensified. "Go home, Jane. Plan your event. I'll see you soon."

She coughed to clear her throat and forced her mind on the matter at hand. Which wasn't Conrad's confession. "Right. See you soon." Too soon. Jane had three days to find the perfect costume with a matching hat, write her script for the tour and spread the word about.

As she stood, she winked and told him, "Don't forget to buy your ticket and pay your out-of-town fee, agent. You won't be allowed in the cemetery otherwise."

"Jane, I doubt anything can keep me away from you."

JANE REELED ALL the way home. Not ponder about Conrad's confession? Impossible. He'd hinted at the big R. At a *relationship*. Getting to know each other. Spending days and nights together. Developing feelings.

Losing everything.

A lump formed in her throat, and she swallowed it back. Nope, it remained. Sweat beaded her brow. Why, why, why did the thought of a murder investigation invigorate her but the thought of caring for someone terrify her? Why couldn't the Ladling women ever fall in love and be happy? Just for a little while?

Deep breath in. Out. Jane pasted on a smile and offered Rolex his preferred greeting. As he purred, the fear faded, and her mind cleared. So much to do! She checked phone messages, looked over the graveyard trust, then sped through the day's security feed. All was well at Garden of Memories. Excellent.

Breathing a sigh of relief, she settled into her living room recliner with Rolex and a laptop to post to the Headliner. After several attempts, she came up with, *Come one, come all!*

Take an adults-only midnight tour of the Garden of Memories. Hunt for ghosts...and gold. Glimpse a murder site... Order tickets today! No ticket, no entry.

Along with the reluctant help of Sheriff Moore, Fiona helped spread the word, passing out the new pamphlets Jane printed.

Each day, she grew giddier. Ticket sales climbed beyond her wildest dreams–and consternation. She'd wanted suspects to attend, not everyone in town. Even Tiffany Hotchkins had signed up. And okay, yes, Jane experienced a twinge of guilt when she imagined discussing the doctor's death with his wife, but sacrifices must be made. A crime had been committed, and someone must be brought to justice.

To Jane's delight, she found the ensemble of the century at Très Chic Consignment. No doubt she would shine for Saturday's performance. A flawless black gown touted as widow weeds. Lace and bustles abounded. She fell in love with the taffeta creation the moment she spotted the pagoda sleeves.

The day of the tour, she donned the garment eagerly. At first.

"Buttons are not for the faint of heart," Fiona muttered from behind her, working another bead through its hole.

They occupied Jane's bedroom. She leaned into a bedpost, still learning to breathe while wearing a corset. No wonder Victorian ladies required fainting couches.

She stared out the far window. A full moon tonight. What could be more perfect?

Throughout the afternoon, she'd caught glimpses of Conrad and Beau setting up more cameras and hanging lanterns to light the way, taking measures to keep her as safe as possible.

"The buttons just...never ...end," her friend huffed.

"Can you imagine doing this every day? And night!" Jane

finished the mother-of-pearl fasteners on her cuffs. "God bless the inventor of zippers."

"Indeed." A pause. Then, "Hon? I want you to be careful tonight, okay? I mean it." The older woman's voice thickened. "You're precious to me, and I promised your grandmother I'd always take real good care of you. Don't go making me a liar, you hear."

"I won't." Her heart squeezed. "I'll be careful. And you'll be careful, too." Fiona would be manning the gate, taking tickets.

"Of course." Her friend cleared her throat. "Now then. The buttons are done, but what are we going to do about the two-foot train? If left free flowing, those pleated edges will snag on the gravestones."

"No worries. The material tucks in to create a triple bustle."

"Oh yes. I see the hooks." Fiona secured the designated fabric in place and patted Jane's shoulder. "There. All done."

"Not quite. Wait until you catch a gander at this." She glided across the room, her shoulders ramrod straight. What was it about an elaborate Victorian gown that changed your attitude along with your posture? She lifted the lid from a hatbox and slowly drew out a six-inch top hat, complete with netting the hue of raven's wings. Were angels singing? "I didn't tell you, because I wanted it to be a surprise, but I finally found it," she said, awe all but dripping from her voice. "*The* hat." A tulle bow. Netting that spilled over the brim and along her nape. What could be better?

Her friend clapped in true delight. "Are you telling me you're done buying hats? That your collection is complete?"

"Don't be silly. Collections can't be completed." Jane turned to study her reflection in the full-length mirror hanging on her wall. She looked incredible, if she did say so herself. Dark hair in a severe knot. Bangs perfect for once. The corset gave her a sultry, hourglass figure.

Motions careful, she secured the hat in place. Oh, wow. Yes. Yes! Even better.

What would Conrad and Beau think? Almost time to find out.

After one final glance in the mirror, she squared her shoulders. "I'm ready."

CHAPTER THIRTEEN

Denise Green
Now I Know Something You Don't.
Plot 858, Garden of Memories

*J*ane looked out over the growing crowd in horror. Considering the number of tickets she'd sold, she'd expected a throng, but this was a mob. People never quit coming. There were far more bodies filling the entrance to the cemetery than tickets sold.

Had the entire population of Aurelian Hills decided to come tonight?

Sadly, no one else had dressed in costume. Well, unless she counted Conrad, and she absolutely did not. Some groundskeeper's helper. He'd arrived in full Georgia Bureau of Homicide regalia, obviously hoping to scare off bad guys. His way of protesting her involvement. He hadn't wanted her to run the tour, after all. Guests continued to cast wary glances his way. Jane only prayed the killer cared more about hiding his or her crime than evading the GBH.

"Did you have to bring the badge?" she whispered to him.

Her nerves were slightly…frayed. At least he and Beau had built a small, makeshift dais to grant her added height. A queen who towered over her subjects. Well, most of her subjects. The two men who flanked her sides towered over *her*.

Conrad stood at her right, the unmissable badge dangling from a chain around his neck. He'd even worn a jacket with GBH emblazoned on the back, the huge letters noticeable from space. Probably glowed in the dark, too. It surprised her to know he'd left his bulletproof vest at home.

"And the gun on your hip? Seriously, Conrad." This was supposed to be somewhat covert. Didn't help that a glowing lantern rested at her feet, light glinting off the metal.

He flashed her a big bad wolf smile. "All the better to protect you with."

Why, why, why did he have to be so shiver inducing? "You've got to dial down your level of menace, at least."

"I want everyone to know I'm here, and I'm watching," he replied, and if anything, he ramped up his threatening stance. She *felt* his challenge: *Try me.*

With a sigh, she shifted her focus to the guests. More people poured into the Garden, one after the other, collecting in the gated entrance that separated the yard from the cemetery. The perfect spot for herding a large group in the direction of her choice. Spacious, spooky with a scattering of gnarled trees, and bathed in golden moonlight.

The night offered the most amazing bouquet of scents. Her favorites. Magnolia and gardenia. Also freshly mowed grass and something she would swear was stardust. Insects buzzed and frogs croaked, creating a lovely symphony she'd enjoyed most of her life. The perfect night. Except it wasn't. Not with a gun-toting special agent and a glaring military hero stationed near her like rabid castle guards.

Although, she supposed Beau's "outfit" did in fact count

as a costume. Conrad had snorted when he'd spotted the other guy for the first time this morning. She'd tried, okay, cobbling together a groundskeeper uniform from stuff her Pops had worn. Sure, males once wore their shorts a little shorter in the 1970s. And the ribbed T-shirt with cuffed short sleeves might not be at the height of fashion, but it was the only piece of clothing she'd found with *Garden of Memories* screen-printed above the pocket.

Truth be told, the thin cotton outlined every muscle of his well-defined chest. Hmm, maybe Beau the fashionista could start a trend. Men displaying more leg, because hello. Too bad neither Eunice nor Ana could make tonight's festivities to see him in all his glory. Apparently Eunice was dealing with some kind of an accounting emergency, and Ana was out of town.

"I hate this," Beau muttered from her left.

"So you've said." She cast him a pointed glance over her shoulder. "Six times."

"Have I mentioned how much I like your new look?" Conrad asked the other man, and yes, there was a snicker in his tone.

Beau crossed his arms, his biceps straining the material. "Shut it. I make bad look good."

"I have the same garments in different colors," she told her agent. "If you'd prefer to be co-groundskeeper for the night, I'll grab them."

"Hard pass," Conrad said.

A stir flowed over the gathering crowd when Tiffany Hotchkins arrived. Raw grief glazed her eyes. She'd anchored her dark bob away from her face. A dirty, wrinkled T-shirt and ripped jeans bagged on her thin frame.

Several townspeople swarmed her, offering condolences. Others merely snuck a peek at the new widow.

Her pain struck Jane as genuine and sparked a massive

uprising of guilt. At that moment, she (lightly) scratched Tiffany off her suspect list, then elbowed Conrad and whispered, "See? It's working. I just got my first big break. I'm now relatively certain there's someone in town who *didn't* do the crime."

Conrad leaned down to whisper in her ear. "This is still a terrible idea."

Such a rich, gravelly, shiver-inducing voice. "You'll change your tune when I solve the entire case later tonight." Boastful words, but dang it, she wanted those bragging rights more than she'd ever wanted anything. And justice or whatever.

"Oh, you're resolving everything tonight, are you?" He didn't try to hide his amusement.

"Yes, sir. I am." Maybe? She watched as Abigail pushed through the crowd to hug her friend. The brunette and the redhead hooked arms to present a united front. Well. Maybe Abigail wasn't the type to betray her friend. *Maybe*. Jane wasn't ready to scratch another name off the list just yet.

More guests poured in.

She greeted each one with a wave. "Hello and welcome to a night sure to haunt your memories for eternity." Oh! Emma had arrived. At her side, her soon-to-be ex Anthony. If they still planned to become exes?

Emma wore all black. She even added black gloves. Ohhhhh. Was the number one suspect planning to go after the crowbar while lost in the shadows tonight, perhaps?

Jane spotted two others from the medical clinic. Dr. Garcia, whose bruising had begun to fade, appeared just as nervous as before. Caroline dressed in a jacket the same unmissable shade of yellow as the letters on Conrad's jacket.

Oh, look. The clinic's receptionist and another nurse. Heck, the clinic could have a staff meeting right now.

Like a game of clue. Who killed the doctor, in the graveyard, with the crowbar?

Caroline glanced her way, offered a small smile, then faced an approaching Dr. Garcia. The two huddled together, not inviting the other employees to join in.

Whispered conversations merged, but Jane's name surfaced again and again. Wait. Conrad's name surfaced, too. Was his presence fueling the rumors about their so-called romance?

Her cheeks burned. Had Conrad heard about her doodles?

The din of the crowd grew louder. Someone bumped into someone else, and a plethora of retorts rang out. Conrad and Beau tensed. Jane's heart pounded. Was a fight about to happen?

Sweat dotted her brow and dampened the material at the small of her back, doubt attacking her from every front. Had she made a terrible mistake? There were too many people here to corral them all. Too many motives and variables she couldn't control.

Her breath shallowed, the corset suddenly cinching her in all the wrong places.

"Jane," Conrad prompted as he moved closer. So close, the front of his body molded to the back of hers. He settled a hand on her hip and bent his head to her ear. "Focus on me. Breathe in. Out. Good. Did I tell you how beautiful you look in that dress? The hat is. …not terrible."

A little laugh barked from her. Her eyes widened. Dang, she liked this man.

"Calm now?" he asked, squeezing her.

Each of her nerve endings pinged. She nodded, then notched her chin. The only mistake she'd made tonight was thinking she'd made a mistake. She had this.

From the town square, a clock tower gonged. Midnight had arrived. The tour could begin.

As she scanned the crowd, she memorized the faces of her attendees. Tons of people would receive a bill tomorrow. Jane planned to use every cent she earned tonight to pay Beau for his work.

"All right, boys. It's showtime." She bent to collect the lantern. The light must have glinted off Conrad's gun again, because several guests paled and hurried to insert themselves into the masses.

Stepping to the edge of the dais, Jane sought everyone's attention. "Welcome, foolish mortals," she called, then exaggerated a wince. "I mean, brave souls. I suggest you gird your loins, for you are soon to meet the spirits that haunt this cemetery, and there's no turning back." With her thumb, she triggered a remote tucked in her pocket. The stringed lights hanging throughout the area blinked to life. A ghostly wind moaned over a hidden speaker.

Someone shrieked, and a few uncomfortable laughs followed. Good. Best to keep everyone guessing. They might reveal more than they'd intended.

"Are you ready to enter into the land of the dead?" Considering she wore miles of fabric, a thousand ruffles and a lung flattening corset, she handed the lantern to Conrad and lifted both of her hands in expectation, whispering to her companions, "Help me!"

After only the briefest pause, each man aided her descent of the steps.

"I'll follow the group from the rear," Beau said before jogging off.

Conrad returned the lantern to Jane. "I'll remain by your side at all times. Don't even think about ditching me."

"Do you hear me complaining?" Like a good hostess—

GENA SHOWALTER & JILL MONROE

guidetress?—Jane swept forward, leading the charge. "Follow me...if you dare."

As the group of what seemed to be millions motored past the gravesites, she shared facts about Aurelian Hills, secret societies and the duels and murders that brought the first occupants to the Garden. She made dramatic hand gestures for effect. And puns. Lots and lots of puns.

Something she quickly learned: she couldn't keep track of the right people while remembering her lines. But she tried, her determination unmatched. Jane stuck to the lighted trail, knowing Beau's cameras recorded everything. Thankfully, the route provided a stunning view. Paper lanterns hung from poles, illuminating headstones. The angel statue cast an arresting shadow. Hanging vines created curtains here and there. Vines swirled beside the cobblestone path.

The first stop on the tour was, as always, an introduction to Muffin. Tonight, though, she wanted the killer to see the fake crowbar and attempt to snatch on camera. As everyone gathered around her, she shifted her attention to Emma as much as possible. Which wasn't possible because she couldn't spot the woman in the crowd. Dr. Garcia and Caroline seemed particularly touched by the ghost dog that watched over the residents. Many others remained uninterested, glancing around. On the hunt for the dead or gold?

Next Jane visited a series of five headstones, each depicting the grim reaper in a different stance. Her audience had thinned, and she fought to hide a grin. Seemed some of her guests had lagged behind or wandered off. How interesting.

"This is the Death family," she said. "And yes, that is their real name, only pronounced Deeth. They liked to poke fun of their unusual name."

"More and more people are branching off," Conrad muttered to her.

"Thank you, Captain Obvious," she muttered right back. Muffin's marker wasn't the only one being watched by cameras. Later, when her last guest left, Jane would watch every stream of feed and find out who had returned to the murder weapon, who had checked out the murder site, and who had inspected the coffins and gravestones with the Order of Seven symbol.

To ensure the right people felt secure enough to venture off, Jane continued on the tour as if nothing was wrong. Except things took a horrible turn after the eighth stop.

Murmurs about the supposed gold grew louder and louder until someone shouted, "Where is it? Show us the gold!"

Other shouts rang out.

"Actually, the Gold family isn't buried here," she said, playing ignorant, "but if you'll look to your right, you'll notice—"

"I found it!" The claim came from a distance and silenced the remaining shouts. "I found where Dr. Hots was murdered!"

Gasps and murmurs sounded, everyone turning to look in the voice's direction. In groups of two and three, her guests broke off, splitting from the crowd. Emma aimed in that direction, too.

"We might as well join them," Jane muttered, barreling forward to lead the stragglers. You never knew when a clue would turn up.

Conrad caught up, maintaining a post at her side.

"How dare you," a woman shrieked. Not just any woman. Tiffany Hotchkins.

Jane and Conrad picked up the pace, reaching plot 39 in record time. Stationary lanterns glowed, illuminating the crowd.

Abigail stood beside Tiffany and pointed a finger in Emma's face. "Haven't you done enough?"

Emma swiped at the tears streaming down her cheeks, her fingers trembling. "I'm sorry. I never meant to hurt you, Tiff. But I loved him too."

People were drawing together, creating a circle around the women. No sign of Anthony. Jane decided to reach an organic conclusion. Conrad must have decided the same, considering he didn't leap to anyone's rescue.

Please, please, please let someone admit something they shouldn't!

A vein pulsed in the widow's forehead, and her hands balled into fists. With a wail, Tiffany Hotchkins launched herself at the nurse. The two hit the ground and rolled. The widow pulled hair and clawed. The nurse merely defended herself.

Okay, so, change of plan. The organic conclusion might be another murder. "No! Stop this!" Jane called. She'd wanted more barbs of information, not a physical altercation.

Conrad acted fast, rushing ahead of her to grab the two combatants and wrench them apart.

Beau arrived a split second later, shooting into the mess to take possession of Tiffany, who fervently fought his hold.

No sign of Sheriff Moore. Jane wondered if he'd stayed behind at the ticket booth for some mysterious reason.

Emma brought her hands to her bleeding face and sobbed. Her gloves had come off, revealing old, scabbed cuts. Jane frowned. Those cuts looked an awful lot like feline scratches. Had the nurse tangled with a cat recently?

A specific cat, perhaps? Two punctures topping two zagged lines.

Breath caught in Jane's throat, blocking her airway. In an instant, she remembered the terror of being unable to locate her baby. The agony of wondering what had happened.

"You did it," Jane gasped out. The motive? Love. An unholy, unexpected rage exploded from her. Her movements slowed. A predator locked on prey, she eased the lantern to the ground. "You're the cat endangerer. That, I know."

"Jane," Conrad grated a few feet away as he struggled to contain Tiffany. "Whatever you're thinking, don't. Stand down."

As if. "The only question now," she continued to Emma, "is whether or not you're the killer." She'd spoken so quietly, no one had heard. In fact, nobody paid any attention to her. Sharper words flew from her tongue. "You were in my house and scared my baby. He could have *died.*" The thought of burying Rolex... "He could have died as terribly as Dr. Hotchkins. Because of you."

Jane erupted, launching at Emma. Those hours of self-defense with Conrad were about to pay off. There wasn't anything he could do to stop her as she plowed into the other woman. They toppled, the nurse ripping from Conrad's grip.

This time, Emma refused to take her medicine. She fought back.

Conrad moved to pull them apart, only to focus on the lawyer after he shoved his way through the crowd. As the agent took down the irate husband, Jane knocked Emma flat on her back, out cold.

Grinning, she wiped her hands together in a job well done. "Someone call Fiona. Tell her what I did. Oh, and maybe round up one of our visiting doctors."

"Dr. Garcia!" multiple voices called. "Whittington!"

"Emma did it," she told Conrad as he forced Anthony to the ground and cuffed his hands behind his back. "She's my intruder. She might be the murderer too!"

"Maybe. I'll question her, I promise you."

Beau maneuvered Tiffany into the same supine position, and zip-tied her wrists.

He just carried the ties in his pocket all casual-like? Okay. Guaranteed Eunice will find that sexy.

Caroline hurried forward. "I'm here, I'm here. Who's my patient?"

"Emma," Jane told her.

The assistant crouched beside the unconscious nurse and checked her vitals. Sweat dotted her brow. She'd ditched her bright jacket, at least. Hey, why had she worn a jacket in the first place? Like so many others, she now wore all black.

Hmm. Had *Caroline* snuck around the cemetery? To what end?

Well. The case wasn't exactly solved, after all. Too bad for Caroline the cameras came with night vision.

"Take her to the clinic without jostling her too much. I haven't found any signs of a concussion, but I'd like to do a more thorough examination," the PA announced.

Hoping to remain with Emma and the physician assistant, gaining privacy for questioning in the process, Jane flattened a hand over her stomach and faked a sharp pain. "Oh no. Was I injured internally during the fight I just won? I should probably get checked out, too."

Conrad glared at her while standing guard over his captives. "I'm sure you'll recover. I can't leave until my team arrives. You'll stay here with me."

"Allow her to suffer with what is clearly a legitimate ailment?" Beau asked with an almost amused tsk-tsk in his voice. "Don't be so cruel, Conrad. I'll drive Jane to the clinic. Since she isn't under arrest, she's free to go. Isn't she?"

Teeth clenched, Conrad grated, "She is."

She tried not to beam her thanks in the midst of her great stomach agony. Did Beau suspect Caroline of wrongdoing, too? Or think she only hoped to stay with Rolex's greatest foe? Or maybe he just liked getting one over on the special agent. Each motive received Jane heartily approval.

Beau scooped Emma into his arms and headed out. Caroline followed him, but Jane lagged before racing to Conrad, who stood behind Anthony and Tiffany. The pair had given up the battle and simply panted while laying on the grass. All around, townsfolk murmured about what they'd witnessed. Tomorrow, Fiona might die of disappointment for missing the event of the century.

Jane rose to her tiptoes and kissed Conrad's stubble-covered cheek. "I'll be fine, I promise." The scent of cedar and spice made her heart trip, a soothing balm like no other.

"You better be." Expression a mix of fear and anger, he said, "I know you consider Emma the killer, and you want to remain by her side. For my peace of mind, stay here."

"Conrad, you don't ask a star to stop shining. You make a wish and hope for the best. And Emma isn't my only reason for going."

His eyes narrowed. "When this is over, I'm placing you under immediate house arrest. Just see if I don't. I'll be your jailer." He tightened his grip. "You'll do everything I tell you for once."

"Maybe," she said, a smile spreading. Her life had certainly gotten infinitely more interesting since meeting this man. She kind of owed the killer a thank you. But only kind of.

From somewhere in the distance, Beau called her name.

"I've got to go," she said. "Listen. Don't be mad, but I think Caroline is guilty of something major. Maybe murder, who knows? But don't worry. I'm gonna get answers. Okay, see ya. Bye!" She raced off to join Beau inside his truck as Conrad sputtered questions at her retreating back.

CHAPTER FOURTEEN

Kosta Diakos
Now The Party Can Start.
Plot 665, Garden of Memories

"*P*ut her right here," Caroline Whittington said as she marched through the clinic.

Beau and Jane followed. A tower of strength at her side, he and his short shorts were streaked with dirt. He carried Emma as gently as possible and eased her onto an exam table. The paper cover crinkled under her legs.

Emma had yet to wake up. Which Jane didn't understand.

Caroline exited, calling, "Come on, Jane. You'll be in here. Beau, stay with Emma and shout if she rouses."

Jane shared a glance with Beau. He was gearing up to protest. To demand he remain at her side. To claim he could zip-tie Emma to the table and all would be well. Except his big, intimidating presence might prevent Caroline from opening up.

"I might need to undress," she told him, not the least bit

flustered by the thought of stripping down in front of her friend. Nope. Not her.

A muscle jumped in his jaw. "I'll turn my back."

Not. The. Least. Bit. "Stay here. You'll only be a shout away," she whispered for his ears alone.

"I only helped you get here so we can put an end to this and get you out of danger, not throw you into more of it."

"One, you need to guard a possible murderer. Two, there's nothing to worry about. Caroline isn't foolish enough to attack me with such a strong, concerned witness nearby. Plus, did you see my savage brawl with Emma? I've got skills, Beau. Good ones."

His brows dropped. So did his voice. "You think Caroline is involved in the murder?"

"Don't you?" Jane left him sputtering as fervently as Conrad as she tracked Caroline to an exam room two doors down. A different room than before, though it possessed the same design.

Did the PA have an affair with Dr. Hots or not? Did she treasure hunt with him, perhaps? Coworkers with mining benefits.

Did Caroline kill him for cheating on her? Or for cheating her of her share of gold? Maybe she was or wasn't the one who'd delivered the fatal blow, but she was absolutely, positively involved in the crime. How could she not be? Her name started with a *C* and Jane wanted to kick herself for not noticing such an obvious clue sooner.

Had Emma committed the murder or merely participated in some way?

"Shut the door behind you." The assistant puttered around the space.

Let's do this. As soon as Jane obeyed, a second order rang out. "Lay down on the table."

Again, Jane obeyed. Not an easy task, considering the bulk of her dress.

"Tell me more about your stomach pains, Jane." Caroline secured her hair in a knot at her nape and tugged a latex glove over each hand.

"Oh, um, to be honest, I'm already feeling better."

"Well, stress can ebb and flow, especially after a traumatic event. And you certainly suffered through a traumatic event tonight, didn't you? Let's make sure you're not feeling simply better because you're in shock."

As Caroline checked her vitals, Jane debated the best way to begin her interrogation.

Then the other woman asked, "Is there any chance you could be pregnant?"

"No," she rushed out, her cheeks heating.

"Are you sure? You might not be far enough along to realize it."

"I'm *very* sure."

Caroline offered her a fleeting smile. "Did you lose consciousness during the fight?" She swiped a pen light off the countertop and flashed it across Jane's eyes. "Your pupils are responding nicely. How's your stomach? Still calm?"

"Correct," she said, doing her best to hide her growing frustration. She'd missed the perfect opportunity to delve into the case. If Jane returned the conversation to Conrad, Caroline might suspect Jane's suspicion.

"That's a good sign." The PA patted her shoulder. "I'm going to palpate your abdomen now. Just want to make sure there's no internal bleeding." She pressed here and there, moving garments as needed. "Do you mind if I ask you a personal question?"

"Not at all." In fact, she eagerly awaited a more personal conversation with the woman.

"I heard you accuse Emma of murdering Dr. Hotchkins."

Jane didn't hear a question, personally or otherwise. "I did that, yes."

"I think you're right."

Okay. Not what she'd expected the other woman to say. "You do?"

"I don't mean to speak ill of a coworker, but her obsession with the doctor was getting out of hand. When we were together, she talked of him and little else. The morning of the murder, I overheard her planning to meet him. I told Special Agent Ryan, right at the beginning, but he did nothing."

Her heart raced. Here it was. Confirmation of her suspicions. Emma. The doctor. Their plans. And yet, her gut wasn't satisfied. Something teased the back of her brain. Was it all a little too easy? Did Caroline come across as a bit desperate? Overcompensating because she feared the truth might catch up to her, perhaps?

Wait. Was that...could it be...? A tiny streak of neon blue stained Caroline's shirt. Oh, sweet goodness, it was!

Caroline had spray painted something at the cemetery. Just like she'd spray-painted the buildings and cars, tagging her own workplace and vehicle to make herself appear to be a victim rather than a perpetrator. If she were capable of that...what else might she do?

Am I about to solve my first case?

Excitement singed Jane's every nerve ending. In the beginning, she had wondered if Conrad considered her twisted enough to do the crime and insert herself into the investigation. She wasn't. But Caroline might be. What if the PA hadn't been accusatory when she and Jane had spoken on the phone? What if she'd been frightened and seeking information about the body or the murder weapon? What if she did all that spray painting to restart rumors about the gold? What if Emma and Caroline had worked together? That would mean the PA had turned on her partner, now that the heat of suspicion blazed hotter.

Now, to get her talking. "I'm sure Con—Special Agent Ryan investigated every lead," Jane told her with a firm tone. "He's very dedicated and super smart. He will stop at nothing to catch the person or persons responsible for this heinous crime. He'll make sure that someone is thrown into the worst prison in existence for daring to trample my—for daring to kill the doctor."

Caroline went as still as a statue, not even seeming to breathe. Just for a moment. Just long enough for Jane's internal alarm to blast off. *She knows I know.*

Jane tightened a fist, ready to swing, and opened her mouth to shout for Beau. But the PA moved with shockingly swift reflexes, flattening a hand over her lips. A sharp prick registered in Jane's neck a split second later, her entire body going weak. Inside her head, dizziness surged. Her vision blurred.

"I didn't want things to end this way." Panic dripped from Caroline's tone. She'd done it. She was the one who had committed the murder. The PA eased the pressure on Jane's mouth, but not before she noticed the tremor. "I only wanted to learn what you knew."

And plant more seeds of doubt about Emma? *Don't fear. Think!*

"Please don't fret. I won't harm you, all right?" Caroline continued. "I'm not a bad person. I'm really not. Before Marcus, I'd never hurt anyone. You're going to sleep for a bit. That's all. Just let it happen. When you wake, I'll be gone. You can pretend this was a terrible dream."

Truth? Lies? She tried to shout for help, but no sound emerged. She fought with all her might. Her limbs refused to cooperate. *Helpless?* No! But no matter what she did, she remained immobile and silent.

"I refuse to go to jail for defending my honor." The self-admitted murderer rushed around the room. Different sounds registered. The rustle of clothing. The squeak of tennis shoes. A clink of...glass? "I loved him. More than I've ever loved anyone. I shouldn't have moved to Aurelian Hills, but those decades old rumors are true. The proof is in the *Gold Fever!* exhibit. I was born to find gold, Jane. Marcus caught me studying between patients. I shared things with him I'd never shared with another. My maps. The code." Bitterness infused her tone. "Why? Why did I do that? All along he planned to steal everything for himself!"

Ohhhh. This happened for love *and* money. Jane had absolutely guessed some of this. Hadn't she? She'd guessed a thousand other things, too, but come on! Give her some credit. You had to explore every angle to find the right one, probably. The fact that Conrad had only been halfway right about the motive, well, Jane could live with that.

Please, let me live with that. How did Caroline even expect to get past Beau?

Beau! Jane *must* warn him of the danger. Fighting...fighting so much harder...her heart slammed against her ribs. "Yew wosh gwet..."

"Mr. Harden," Caroline called with a frantic tone. "Help me! Something's wrong with Jane!"

"Nnnn," she tried to shout.

The door immediately opened, hinges squeaking.

"She's having trouble breathing, and I can't get her dress off her. Help me save her and get that corset off her body."

Jane sensed his presence at her side. His head and his clean scent. His strong fingers working her gown. Fighting... a finger moved.

"Jane," he cried. "Stay with me. Something's wrong with her, Dr. Whitting—"

An intake of breath. A heavy thud. No, no, no. Beau had just hit the floor, hadn't he, as drugged and helpless as Jane?

"I'm sorry. I really am," Caroline said, confirming her worst fears. Once again, the PA puttered about. She moved at a more harried clip, opening and closing cabinets. Taking things she might need? "This is all Marcus's fault. His stupid affairs! He owed so much money. Did you know he was being blackmailed *and* paying secret child support?"

No. And dang Conrad to heck for not telling her. A second finger twitched. Then a third. *I can do this!*

"I never should have told him what I'd found at the cemetery," Caroline continued. "Never should have invited him to help me search for more. Why did Emma have to walk into the room that day? She and her swaying ponytail ruined everything! *He* ruined everything." A laugh, just as bitter as her words. "If he'd just kept his word to me, none of this would have ever happened. I had a right to my anger!"

Anger? No. Rage. A moment of rage had ruined the woman's life. Well, and Dr. Hotchkins's.

What would have happened if Jane had killed Emma when she'd lashed out about Rolex? Her stomach twisted. Lesson learned. Control mattered.

"I did everything right. I got rid of Garcia for the day and took your appointment. I fed you information, weaving in enough misdirection. The symbol should have worked. The posts should have worked. I gave them too many suspects to ever pick just one. Convincing Emma to break into your home and visit Fiona should have worked. I could have lived my life the way I always dreamed. Now I'm forced to start over. Again."

Jane's hand curled into a fist. The haze over her eyes dulled, bits of color coming into view. With great effort, she angled her head. Yes, Beau lay sprawled on the floor. Caroline stood near the door, zipping a bag.

A crash sounded, startling the PA, who dropped the bag and stumbled back.

"Jane!"

Conrad. Her heart leaped and flipped.

"Help," she managed to gasp out. She even pulled herself into an upright position and drew the other woman's attention.

With a cry, Caroline swiped up a pair of stitch cutters from the cart and darted behind Jane. As a furious Conrad barreled into the room, a gun in hand and a second agent at his heels, the murdering PA pressed the scissors against Jane's carotid.

Panic flared as Conrad took aim. Jane could only sit there, her body not fully her own to command. She gazed at the pallid Conrad, who'd never looked so fierce or terrified.

He kept his weapon raised and rock steady. "Let her go. Hurting her will only make things worse for you."

Panting now, Caroline pressed the tip in deeper, drawing a bead of blood. The sharp prick surprised Jane. A warm droplet trickled down her neck. "I'm leaving with her. I'll drop her off somewhere once I'm safe."

"No, ma'am, you are not leaving here. There is *no* scenario where I will allow you to harm her and escape, either," Conrad stated calmly. "Letting her go is your best chance of having a future."

Still fighting. At last, the rest of Jane's muscles revived, tingling back to life. What's more, the drugs were wearing off. She could move with a bit more ease, but she didn't. Not yet.

"Conrad," she breathed, and his gaze darted to her. There and back, then there again. Because she smiled, her fear fading as strength returned to her limbs. "I've got this. Trust me."

Remembering everything he'd taught her, she slammed

the back of her head into the PA's face while latching onto her wrist and pushing. Caroline stumbled, losing her balance and dropping the scissors.

And in a snap, the day was saved. Conrad raced over to subdue and cuff the woman, right next to a twitching Beau. His gaze returned to her and narrowed. Relief waged war with fury in their depths.

"Radio for an ambulance," he told the other agent.

"Already done," was the reply. "They'll be here in less than five."

"You and Beau will be checked out without argument," he told Jane. "When the other agents arrive, I'll pass off the PA and find you. Tonight we talk."

CHAPTER FIFTEEN

Vincent Hernandez
I Give This Place Zero Stars.
Plot 2300, Garden of Memories

"Oh my goodness, look at you." Fiona rushed over to hug Jane as she and Beau trudged inside the cottage. "A torn, dirt-streaked dress. Missing beadwork. Dried blood on the material. No hat?"

Oh no! She'd lost *the* hat without even realizing it?

Jane hugged her right back, clinging. "I'm fine. I promise."

Fiona hugged Beau next. "And you, young man? How are you?"

"Despite my stinging pride, I'm all good," he told her with the first hint of a bemused smile. Not used to having someone fuss over him?

"So. Jane's fine, and you're good. Neither one of you have an excuse for not telling me everything that happened the second you entered this house." The best pancake maker in the world glanced between them. "Well? Let's hear it."

Despite the obscenely early morning hour, her friend

hadn't slept a wink, had she? "I will, promise." She hooked an arm through Fiona's and Beau's and led them to the kitchen. "After you feed me."

"How about you tell me while I cook? But only because Conrad has kept me mostly up to date." The other woman offered the information casually, as if she hadn't just rocked Jane's world.

"He has? How? When? You tell *me* everything," she insisted.

Fiona fluffed her hair, clearly thrilled to know more than anyone else. "Well, he told me about the fight and your quote unquote secret wish to spend the rest of your life in personal lockup and total lack of personal safety awareness." After Jane and Beau plopped into chairs at the table, Fiona poured them a glass of sweet tea. "He mentioned Caroline Whittington's involvement and subsequent confession. Emma's confession. The Order of Seven. Your trip to the hospital. And finally, how you both got the all clear from the doctor."

Caroline hadn't lied about the drug she had used. A neuromuscular blocking agent for general anesthesia, with no lasting side effects.

Rolex came prancing around a corner and hopped onto the table. He sat in the empty bowl centerpiece Jane kept just for him. She scratched behind his ears.

"Here I am cooking," Fiona said, puttering around. "Tell me your side of the story. Conrad, as helpful as he's been, left out the most critical details." A teasing sparkle entered her dark eyes. "I'm wondering how the nurses at the hospital reacted to your shorts, Beau. Jane's grandpa never looked so...tightly packed."

Pink stained his cheeks, and Jane pressed a hand over her mouth to silence what would no doubt be a ridiculous giggle.

"I tried not to notice what *anyone* thought of my shorts," he grumbled.

The giggle escaped, despite her best efforts, and there was no stopping it. Soon, Fiona and Beau joined in the laughter as well. When Jane's gaze connected with Beau's, he stopped laughing. His eyes blazed.

She gulped. He, um, really valued their friendship, huh?

"The nurses were overjoyed with Beau. Fussed over him as if he were a delicate baby bird," Jane said, missing Conrad. "Now tell me everything else Conrad told you." Even though she was an official, nonofficial crime-solving genius detective, Jane wasn't above bribery. "Take your own advice and leave nothing out."

In her element—gossip—Fiona dropped a stick of butter on the counter and rubbed her hands together. "Well. Caroline fancies herself a modern-day gold hunter. Apparently, the Order of Seven brought her to town. She deciphered some codes in the journals at the museum and learned of the second set of hidden cemetery gold. She also fell in love with Dr. Hots. He pursued her, hoping to use her for the gold."

That, Jane had already learned. But one detail confused her. "What did so many women see in the guy?"

"I asked Conrad the same thing. He says the doctor mostly picked married women who were less likely to tattle, with the occasional single gal thrown into the mix." Fiona leaned over and propped her chin on her hands. "Caroline learned the truth about his intentions at the same time the nurse discovered his philandering ways. She began plotting right away, spray-painting the fleur-de-lys on buildings and cars and posting on the Headliner anonymously to spread rumors about the gold. She figured more gold hunters meant more suspects. She even slipped specific information to Dr. Hotchkins, which drove him to dig up the grave on his own, hoping to keep the money for himself. Meanwhile, Caroline hid nearby and struck at the perfect moment."

Smart. "After Caroline drugged me, she admitted she convinced Emma to break into my house. Do you know how they copied my key or what excuse she used to convince Emma to do it?"

"Apparently Caroline copied your key weeks ago. Back when you were a one-woman show, caring for an endless stretch of land without any security measures in place," Fiona chided. "In her free time, she's been casing the place, learning our habits. All very clandestine."

What! "I never knew." Never even suspected. And Jane (apparently) suspected everyone of everything!

"Don't worry," Beau said. "It won't be happening again."

"Of course it won't." Fiona came over to give his hand a comforting pat. "Now, where was I? Oh yes." She rested a hand on her hip. "Caroline stopped coming once you installed the cameras. She convinced Emma that Dr. Hots was having an affair with you too, Jane, and that he'd stashed compromising photos and videos of Emma out here. A way to make the nurse more of a suspect."

Well. No wonder Emma had been so rude during Jane's appointment. "What about Anthony Miller? What part did he play?"

"He came with Emma to help her steal those photos and videos that don't exist. Oh!" Fiona brightened and clapped. "Conrad asked me to do him a favor, and you'll never guess what, Jane." Without pause, she blurted out, "He asked for my famous blueberry pancakes! That's the real reason I offered to cook for you. Not because I love you more than life itself."

Joy washed over Jane. Could this night get any better? "Then why aren't you cooking, woman?"

Her friend laughed and padded back to the kitchen to

finish gathering the necessary supplies. "So? Tell me! Did anyone find any gold?"

"Not a speck," Beau said.

"Well..." Jane nibbled on her bottom lip. "Caroline did discover some." The PA's exact words: *I never should have told him what I'd found at the cemetery.* "Whatever she found, she found before Dr. Hots dug up plot 39."

Fiona stopped seasoning the pan, a stick of butter in one hand and a spatula in the other. "I'd heard the rumors, of course, but I never thought... I mean, if there was gold out here, your Pops would have ferreted it out. I swear that man could find a penny in a mud puddle."

Beau leaned toward Jane, his gaze dead serious. "You require full-time security. And a dog. Or three. Big ones. The toughest street mutts at the pound."

"Agreed," Fiona said, wagging the spatula in her direction.

"Well, Rolex has gotta agree as well and I don't think that'll happen." Jane shrugged, all *what can you do?* "Since my tours are such huge earners now, I can afford to pay someone a semidecent wage. Do you happen to know anyone who's looking for—"

"No need to search," he interjected, then tipped his glass to his lips and drained his tea. Ice clinked together. "I accept the position."

"Sorry, but you don't get the job." She meant that with every fiber of her being. "You haven't taken a cent for your previous hard work. You tear up my IOUs and refuse to give me itemized bills."

His expression turned...what the heck was that look? He'd never radiated such determination.

"Very well." Beau stood and, without another word, stalked off.

Um. What? Jane and Fiona locked eyes. "What just

GENA SHOWALTER & JILL MONROE

happened?" She didn't know about her friend, but she kind of felt like a raccoon caught in a trashcan who'd just been illuminated by a car's headlights.

"Will he come back?" Fiona whispered.

"I don't know." But oh, she hoped so. She really liked having him in her life.

But he did return several minutes later, with a pen and piece of paper in hand. He reclaimed his seat and slid the paper Jane's way. Confused, she glanced down. What the...? A handwritten bill for services rendered. Except he'd listed only the benefits *Jane* had given him.

Things Jane Has Done for Beau:

- Talks about setting him up on dates, but never delivers—$50,000
- Time with Rolex—Negative 1 Million Dollars
- Hats—Negative 2 Million Dollars
- The feast—8 Billion Dollars
- The View—Everything I own
- The Smiles—Priceless

Jane blinked back tears and swallowed. Then swallowed again. When she'd first reconnected with Beau, he'd been unable to relax. So much tension had radiated off the man, it had inspired her quest to find him a girlfriend and a buddy— she planned to set him up with Eunice or Ana. And yet, *Jane* was the one who'd given him the gift of a smile. Laughter, too. She'd even helped him relax. If she could do it, anyone could.

The fine lines around his eyes were no longer etched as deep. Not constantly, anyway. His spine had softened, no more a rod of unbending steel. This was exactly what she'd dreamed for him. Only better. Because they were friends, and there was nothing better. Ladling didn't lose friends to curses.

Now, her goal for him shifted. He deserved more relaxation and laughter. He deserved a happily ever after. And Jane could help him find it. With the case solved, that double date might even happen next weekend.

"For your information," she said when she found her voice. "Time with Rolex is worth at least a million on the plus side."

He gave her a look that conveyed a clear message: *You know better.* "I was being generous with the negative million."

She tried to maintain a stern expression but laughed. "Fine! You're hired. But this time I *am* paying you, and you *are* accepting every dime, and you are *not* ripping up the checks. The moment you stop taking my money, you're fired."

He opened his mouth to argue but changed his mind. "I don't need the money," he grumbled.

He didn't? Well, well. A new mystery to solve. "I don't care, Beau. No pay, no work. I mean it."

"Fine," he said, echoing her agreement.

"Now that that's settled, why don't you two go wash up and change into clean clothes. I need a few moments of privacy to add my secret ingredient," Fiona said, mixing and heating her brown sugar butter syrup in a pot. "Beau, you're staying the night, of course. Or morning. Whatever. You're sleeping here. Feel free to raid the closet in the guest room. That's where I've stored Gary's other shorts."

His cheeks turned bright red again. "I'm good. As Jane can attest, I always keep spare clothes in my truck."

She lost track of their conversation as her mouth watered. Mmm. Vanilla teased her nose. Leave the kitchen when she was mere minutes away from tasting pancake heaven? She nearly whimpered, but she followed Fiona's request anyway. She and Beau stood and shared a soft smile before branching off in different directions. He jogged outside while she flew up the stairs.

During the fastest shower of all time, Jane was careful not to wet her bandage. As the warm water rained over her, she noticed cuts and bruises she must have received during her battle royale with Emma. Aches and pains began to make themselves known too, muscles protesting.

She yawned as she dressed in a soft fitted white tee and flowing pajama pants and stuffed her feet into her favorite house shoes: kitten heads bobbed with every step. Her eyes burned with fatigue, her adrenaline crashing fast. Suddenly she only wanted to crawl under her covers and sleep for days.

Miss those blueberry pancakes? Never! And okay, yeah, maybe she hoped to see Conrad, too. Where was he?

Jane descended the stairs, deep in thought. She'd been separated from the agent for six hours. That was six hours too long! She really, really, really needed to see him again. To burrow against his strong chest and breathe him in. To finally utilize her bragging rights. She'd identified the killer before he had, and she had every intention of rubbing the information in his face.

Fiona had just turned off the burner as Jane soared into the kitchen, unable to stop smiling. Beau had beat her there and already occupied his chair. Rolex hadn't moved from his spot in the center, glaring at the man who'd invaded his house. Jane stopped, just stopped, and drank in the sight. What a beautiful family. A sight she wouldn't mind viewing every day for the rest of her life.

And Conrad? Did she want to add him to the picture forever? Would the Ladling curse ever lift?

A knock sounded at the door. A hard double-rap, and her breath caught. Conrad! She would bet hard earned money on it. Who else nearly beat down a door with a simple double tap?

Beau made to rise, but Jane waved him down.

"Let me," she said, already turning. Fueled by adrenaline once again, she skipped to the front room, her steps suddenly lighter. Then, he was there, right in front of her, nothing but cedar and spice between them.

Their gazes locked, a thrill of awareness zooming through her. His arms were spread, one hand on each side of the door frame. Like Jane, he'd showered and changed. His dark hair was still damp, the strands sticking out in spikes. Had he rushed over immediately afterward?

"Hello, Conrad."

"Hello, sweetheart." He ran his heating gaze over her and smiled slowly, a little wickedly. "Are you ready for our talk?"

Up Next:
Fifty Shades of Grave
Book 2 in the Jane Ladling Mystery Series

ABOUT GENA SHOWALTER

Gena Showalter is the New York Times and USA TODAY bestselling author of multiple "unputdownable" series in paranormal, contemporary, and young adult romance.

Learn more about Gena, her menagerie of rescue dogs, and all her upcoming books at genashowalter.com

ALSO BY GENA SHOWALTER

Immortal Enemies

Start with: Heartless

.

Rise of the Warlords

Start with: The Warlord

.

Lords of the Underworld

Start with: The Darkest Night

.

White Rabbit Chronicles

Start with: Alice in Zombieland

.

Tales of an Extraordinary Girl

Start with: Playing with Fire

.

Everlife

Start with: Firstlife

.

Original Heartbreakers

Start with: The Secret Fling

.

Angels of the Dark:

Start with: Wicked Nights

.

Otherworld Assassins

Start with: Last Kiss Goodnight

.

Non-Fiction:

(Co-written with Jill Monroe)

All Write Already

All Write Already Workbook (coming soon)

The Write Life

.

Gena's Complete List of Releases:

GenaShowalter.com/books

ABOUT JILL MONROE

Jill Monroe is the international best selling author of over fifteen novels and novellas. Her books are available across the globe and *The Wrong Bed: Naked Pursuit* has been adapted for the small screen for Lifetime Movie Network.

When not writing, Jill makes her home in Oklahoma with her husband, enjoys daily walks with her dog Zoey, texting with her two daughters who are away at college and collecting fabric for items she'll sew poorly.

Learn more about Jill at jillmonroewrites.com

ALSO BY JILL MONROE

Sworn Series:

Sworn Promises

Sworn Duty

Sworn By A Kiss

Sworn Protector

.

Wrong Bed Series

Naked Thrill

Naked Pursuit*

*(Now a movie from Lifetime Movie Network)

.

From Hallmark:

At The Heart of Christmas

.

Non-Fiction:

(Co-written with Gena Showalter)

All Write Already

All Write Already Workbook (coming soon)

The Write Life

.

Jill's Complete List of Releases:

jillmonroewrites.com/books

Made in the USA
Monee, IL
04 April 2022

93963496R00113